Children of the
Longhouse

Joseph Bruchac

DIAL BOOKS FOR YOUNG READERS

NEW YORK

Published by Dial Books for Young Readers
A Division of Penguin Books USA Inc.
375 Hudson Street
New York, New York 10014

Text copyright © 1996 by Joseph Bruchac
All rights reserved
Designed by Karen Robbins
Map and chart by Laszlo Kubinyi
Printed in the U.S.A.

First Edition
3 4 5 6 7 8 9 10

Library of Congress Cataloging in Publication Data
Bruchac, Joseph, 1942–
Children of the longhouse / by Joseph Bruchac.
p. cm.
Includes bibliographical references.
Summary: Eleven-year-old Ohkwa'ri and his twin
sister must make peace with a hostile gang of older boys
in their Mohawk village during the late 1400's.
ISBN 0–8037–1793–8. — ISBN 0–8037–1794–6 (lib. bdg.)
1. Mohawk Indians — Juvenile fiction.
[1. Mohawk Indians — Fiction.   2. Indians of North America — Fiction.
3. Brothers and sisters — Fiction.   4. Twins — Fiction.]   I. Title.
PZ7.B82816Ch 1996 [Fic]—dc20 95–11344 CIP AC

For the children of the longhouse—
past, present, and future.

THE GREAT LEAGUE OF PEACE
OF THE IROQUOIS NATIONS
The Longhouse People

SENECA
People of the Hill

CAYUGA
*Marshy Land
People*

ONONDAGA
Firekeepers

ONEIDA
*Standing Stone
People*

MOHAWK
*Flint Nation
People*

MOHAWK

WHITE FLINT
VILLAGE
primarily Wolf Clan

KANATSIOHAREKE
VILLAGE
primarily Bear Clan

BIG FALLS
VILLAGE
primarily Turtle Clan

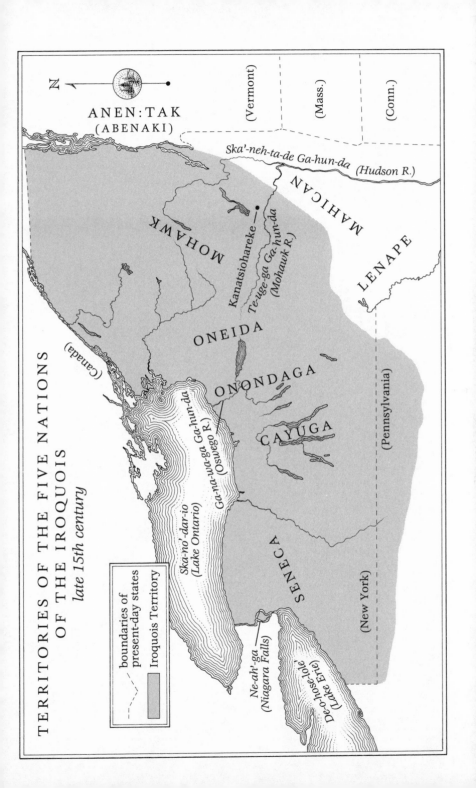

TERRITORIES OF THE FIVE NATIONS
OF THE IROQUOIS
late 15th century

N

ANEN:TAK
(ABENAKI)

(Vermont)

(Mass.)

(Conn.)

Ska'-neh-ta-de Ga-hun-da (Hudson R.)

MAHICAN

MOHAWK

Kanatsiohareke

Te-uge-ga Ga-hun-da
(Mohawk R.)

LENAPE

ONEIDA

ONONDAGA

(Canada)

CAYUGA

Ska-no'-dar-io
(Lake Ontario)

Ga-na-wa-ga Ga-hun-da
(Oswego R.)

(Pennsylvania)

SENECA

(New York)

Ne-ah'-ga
(Niagara Falls)

De-o-hose'-tote
(Lake Erie)

boundaries of
present-day states

Iroquois Territory

Part One
The Way of Peace

1

GRABBER'S PLAN

Ohkwa'ri

*H*is hands pressed on the hard earth of the hillside, Ohkwa'ri felt the footfalls of people coming before he heard or saw them. He leaned forward and looked through the branches of the shrub oak which were green with leaves. Several people were coming up the trail. He recognized the one who led them. It was Grabber.

From his shaded hiding place where he had dug out the loose earth under a slanting slab of stone, Ohkwa'ri could see out through the branches and not be seen. He had crawled in to get out of the hot noon rays of the bright sun of the Strawberry Moon, that time of the year when the days are the longest. This hiding place was his own and no one else's. The little cave and the hill on the other side of the river from his busy village were the two spots where he always came to think. No one knew about this cave except for his sister Otsi:stia, whom he trusted with everything.

Ohkwa'ri thought to crawl out. But for some reason, though his mind thought of showing himself, his body held back. Then Grabber began to speak to his friends, and Ohkwa'ri knew that it was good he had not allowed himself to be seen. The things that Grabber was saying, here on the hillside far above their village, were not things that he wanted anyone to overhear. Grabber was talking about starting a war.

When Ohkwa'ri was very small, he had admired Grabber, who was five winters older than him. Grabber was straight-limbed and very strong. He was the fastest runner of all the young men, a hard worker, and a good hunter. He was the best at all of the games the young men played. Whether it was the game of *Tekwaarathon* in the spring, when they caught the hard deerskin ball in their webbed sticks and ran back and forth on the playing field to score goals, or snow snake in the winter, when they threw their long, finely carved spears down an ice trough to watch them skitter great distances, Grabber was almost always the first among the young men. Because of that he had a loyal group of close friends, and he was always praised for his abilities.

Now that Ohkwa'ri had seen eleven winters, he no longer admired Grabber in the same way. Despite his physical abilities, Grabber was impatient. Although he usually won, he sulked on the few times when he lost. He often had an angry look on his face, and he did not listen well to the advice of the older men. He always thought his own way of doing things for the good of the people was the best.

"Those Anen:taks," Grabber was saying, "those eaters of bark are not real men. They are cowards. We are real human beings. If our fathers and our uncles were not too old and tired, they would see this clearly."

"That is true," said Greasy Hair. Greasy Hair was always at Grabber's side, ready to do whatever his friend suggested.

A small village of the Anen:taks was just over the mountain pass, three days' journey upriver from the big falls and then an equal number of days' journey up the big lakes. Although there were more Anen:taks in all their scattered villages than there were Longhouse People, the Anen:tak villages were often quite small—smaller than those of the Longhouse People and thus easier to raid.

"We should raid them," Grabber said, "because they have not traded fairly with us."

Even though Grabber's statement was not true, Greasy Hair agreed loudly. *"Henh!"* he said.

"When will we make the raid on their village?" asked a third person's voice. From his hiding place under the shelf of rock Ohkwa'ri could not see that person. Grabber was sitting right in front of the cave and his back blocked Ohkwa'ri's view of the others. But he recognized the slow, growling voice. It was Eats Like a Bear, the biggest of all the young men in the village and another of Grabber's three constant companions.

Now, Ohkwa'ri thought, Falls a Lot will ask that same question if he is also here.

Sure enough, the next voice to speak was that of the rather slow-thinking young man who almost always repeated the same questions asked by his friends.

"Yes," said the voice of Falls a Lot, "when will we make the raid on their village?"

Grabber looked around. For a moment his eyes rested on the hidden entrance of the cave, and Ohkwa'ri's heart beat faster. Ohkwa'ri remembered a story that Otsi:stia had told him during the winter, the story of a boy who accidentally overheard a group of two-hearted people who had made an old man sick through their bad magic.

The two-hearted people did not see that boy hidden in the spruce tree, Ohkwa'ri thought. So Grabber will not see me here. He will look away.

Grabber looked back toward his friends.

"We will make the raid while the festival to thank the strawberries is going on. While the people are dancing, we will strike the enemy!"

When the four young men had gone back down the hill, Ohkwa'ri came out of his cave. He was very troubled by the words they had spoken. It was true that the Anen:taks were a different nation. It was true that they spoke a language strange to the people of the Flint Nation. But it was also true that they were now at peace.

Once the Anen:taks had been their enemies, but now the people of the Flint Nation often traded with them. Each year, after the corn harvest, people from Ohkwa'ri's village would travel to the meeting place on the other side of the big south-flowing river, *Ska'neh-ta-de Ga-hun-da*, The River Beyond the Openings. One thing in particular that they liked were the fine canoes of birch bark made by the Anen:taks.

In the old days, before meeting the Anen:taks, the canoes of the Five Nations of the Longhouse People had always been made of elm bark. The Anen:taks taught them how to make birch bark canoes. Yet even though they knew how to make canoes of birch bark, it seemed as if the most beautiful and the fastest canoes were always those made by the Anen:tak people themselves. Although they would never be as close to Ohkwa'ri's people as the four nations which, with his Flint Nation People, made up their Great League of Peace, the Anen:taks respected the people of the Flint Nation and honored the peace. Until now all the people of the Flint Nation had returned that respect and kept that peace.

Ohkwa'ri thought he understood why those three

other young men were in agreement with Grabber's plan. They were impatient. They had not been successful in gaining the respect they thought they deserved. It seemed clear that none of them would ever be a *Roia:ne,* a leader of men, or a Faith Keeper. Nor was it likely that any of them would ever become a Pine Tree Chief, chosen to sit in council with the *Roia:ne.* There was no sign that Grabber or any of the others who followed his lead were wise enough or careful enough to hold such a position of honor. So they had decided to make their names by doing great deeds in a war that no one else wanted.

The words that Grabber had spoken continued to trouble Ohkwa'ri as he walked across the hill toward the strawberry fields, where he knew his sister and the other women would still be gathering berries. The festival to thank the strawberries would begin the next morning.

His own first impulse was to find the four larger boys and confront them. He would tell Grabber and his friends that their hotheaded idea was wrong. No one should break the Great Peace without a good reason, or go to war without the agreement of all the people. But then Ohkwa'ri remembered what his twin sister had told him just the day before.

"Brother," Otsi:stia had said, "you must sometimes think before you do things."

Otsi:stia understood things better than he did. He

had trusted her thoughts before and he would do so now.

The strawberry fields were a wide expanse of meadow not far from the river. The people kept that area clear by burning it each autumn before the snows returned. As a result there were always many strawberry plants. At this time of the year those red berries, each shaped like a little heart, glowed like embers in the new grass. There were many girls and women still picking, although Ohkwa'ri could see that some were already heading back up the trail to the big longhouse, carrying baskets that had been filled with many berries.

It was easy to locate Otsi:stia. As soon as Ohkwa'ri had come to the edge of the fields, she had looked up and raised a hand in greeting. Because they were twins, they always seemed to be able to find each other. It was that way, Herons Flying explained to them, because their minds had started their journey together even before they were born. They would always be close to each other on whatever road they traveled.

Because Herons Flying was their mother, the twins knew that her words were surely true. Although Ohkwa'ri was a finger's width taller and more muscular than his sister, and although her face was a bit more delicate than his, they looked like reflections of each other.

Ohkwa'ri walked carefully across the field, making

sure not to step on any of the berries. The strawberries were everywhere, the three-leafed stalks raising up thick clusters of red and green berries. He knelt down by his sister. He saw that she was almost through picking. Her basket, which she had made from a large piece of elm bark folded up on the sides and then sewn together with the stringy inner bark of the basswood, was almost filled to the brim with berries.

But not every berry found its way into the basket. Her mouth was almost as stained with berry juice as were her fingers. Otsi:stia looked at Ohkwa'ri as if reading her brother's thoughts. She held out a double handful of berries to him.

"Here, Brother," she said, "these may bring a smile to your face."

Ohkwa'ri took the berries and began to eat them. They were as warm and sweet as the scented breeze that was blowing across the fields. But he did not smile as he ate them. He was too deeply troubled.

Otsi:stia studied his face.

"Will you tell me what is bothering you or do I have to guess?" she said with a smile.

Ohkwa'ri looked around. No one was close enough to hear what he and his sister were saying.

"It is Grabber," he said. "He and his followers are planning to make a raid."

Otsi:stia's smile vanished. She put down her basket

of berries and leaned closer to Ohkwa'ri. "Tell me how you know this, Brother," she said.

Ohkwa'ri told her what he had heard while in his cave on the hill. He felt much better as he told it to his sister. She was better at thinking about such things.

"I understand," Otsi:stia said when he finished. "You were right not to confront them. This time you thought before acting, and that is good. Sometimes things happen that you do not expect. Grabber is so hotheaded that he and his friends would have beaten you badly and left you on the hillside. Then they would have gone on their raid before anyone could stop them. Now we must go and tell our grandmother. She will know what to do."

Their grandmother, She Opens the Sky, was the oldest of the three Clan Mothers of the big longhouse. As the oldest woman of the Bear Clan, it was her job to help everyone follow the right path. Everyone respected her for the even-tempered way in which she did this. As Clan Mother she was one of those who chose the clan's leaders. Those Good Men, those *Roia:ne,* would represent the people who made up their village, not only in their councils with the other two clans of the Flint Nation, but also in the great meetings of their League of Five Nations, which took place at Onondaga. There the fifty men—each chosen by a Clan Mother, each chosen to speak for peace, to keep good minds as they spoke—would gather around the central council fire.

The names of the *Roia:ne* were always kept within their clans and passed on when they died or gave up their office. These men could never go to war, never kill another human being, never steal. If any of them ever did so, they would lose their position and their name would be given to someone else. There were always fifty. It had been that way since the founding of the League of Peace. Of those fifty men leaders who maintained their League of Peace, nine came from the Flint People. And of those nine, three came from the Bear Clan. Their mother's brother, Shosko-haro'wane, The Big Tree, was one of those three *Roia:ne*.

She Opens the Sky was sitting outside the great longhouse when Ohkwa'ri and Otsi:stia found her. She was making the strawberry drink that would be shared the following day during the thanksgiving. As a Clan Mother, one of her responsibilities was to see that the people of the village were well fed during the times of ceremony. She did not stop crushing the red berries with her wooden pestle, but she listened closely to the words the two young people spoke.

"Wahe'," she said when they finished. "It is good that you told me this." She looked into Ohkwa'ri's face. "Will you repeat your words in front of Grabber and his followers?"

"*Henh,*" Ohkwa'ri said without hesitation. "Yes, Grandmother."

"That is good, Grandson," She Opens the Sky said. "Now go and tell your uncle Big Tree that I wish to speak with him."

The sun was only the width of two hands away from the end of the day when the council meeting was called to discuss the matter. It was held outside, beneath the great oak tree that grew at the edge of the field downriver from the great longhouse. The three *Roia:ne* sat together on one side of the fire with Ohkwa'ri next to them. Grabber and his three friends stood in front of them on the other side of the fire. In a great circle all around them, the many people of the village were gathered. Of the four young men who had planned to start a war, only Grabber still looked defiant. Eats Like a Bear looked as if he had eaten something that made him sick. Greasy Hair had a look on his face like that of a rabbit who has suddenly seen a fox, and Falls a Lot's knees were shaking. Grabber, though, stood straight and tall.

Looking at Grabber, Ohkwa'ri found that he still had some admiration for the older youth. Grabber did not have any sisters who could help him learn patience. Grabber's father had been killed while on a raid when Grabber was a small boy. Because Grabber had no uncles, he did not have any close male relative to help him learn how to be a man.

Perhaps, Ohkwa'ri thought, that is why Grabber is always trying so hard to be the best at everything.

"Ohkwa'ri," a voice said.

Ohkwa'ri turned to see who had spoken. It was his father, Dagaheo'ga, The One Who Has Two Ideas. Two Ideas was one of the men who acted as a war captain when it was necessary for the people to fight. He was sitting with the *Roia:ne* at this meeting because it concerned the threat of war.

"It is your turn to tell what you heard," Two Ideas said.

Ohkwa'ri stood and took a deep breath. "When I was on the hill back there, Grabber came with his companions. They sat down to talk of a plan. They did not see me. Their plan was to make a raid on the village of the Anen:tak people. They planned to do this tomorrow while the people were dancing. I saw Grabber and I heard the voices of his friends Eats Like a Bear, Greasy Hair, and Falls a Lot. Those four were the ones who agreed to go to war."

Big Tree looked at the four young men who still stood on the other side of the fire. Only Grabber looked back at him.

"I ask you," said Big Tree, "is this true?"

Grabber lifted his chin up and spoke in a loud voice. "It is true," he said. Although his voice shook slightly, his words were spoken clearly.

Once again Ohkwa'ri felt admiration for Grabber. He would not deny his plans. Honor was too important to him, and it was to win honor for himself as a leader in battle that he had thought to make his fool-hardy raid.

"Hear me, you young men," Big Tree said. "Your plan to make a raid was foolish in many ways. It was foolish because you have no experience in war, and it is likely that some or all of you would have been hurt or even killed. Those Anen:tak people are good fighters. It was also foolish because such a raid would have angered the Anen:taks. They would have raided us in turn, and innocent people in our village would have suffered. We are at peace with the Anen:taks now, and because this is a peace that we made with them, it would seem that we have no honor if we were to be the ones to break that peace. But the most foolish thing about your plan was this. . . ."

Big Tree paused and waited, until one by one the three other young men raised their heads to look at him. "The most foolish thing," he continued, "was that you planned this raid on your own. Have you never heard it said that the path to war must go first through the lodge of peace? This is always our way. Our Clan Mothers and the *Roia:ne* must always be consulted first, and then all of the people must agree."

Big Tree looked over to the place where She Opens the Sky sat with the other elder women. She gestured for Big Tree to continue. His words were expressing the thoughts of the Clan Mothers.

"Now," Big Tree said, "since you thought to go to war, hear our War Captain." He looked over at Two Ideas and then sat down.

When Two Ideas stood, Ohkwa'ri felt proud of his father. Two Ideas was not as tall as Big Tree, but he was broader and more muscular. Although he walked and spoke more slowly than Big Tree, Two Ideas could move quickly when he wanted—as quickly as a snapping turtle shooting its head out of its shell. And when Two Ideas grabbed hold of something, he did not let it go. That was also why he was such a good hunter. Whenever he started out on the trail, he would not give up until he caught the game he was after.

Two Ideas walked slowly toward the four young men. He held his fighting club in his right hand. That club was a terrible weapon and was usually kept stored in the elm bark box under his bed in the big longhouse. The end of its curved handle, which was the length of a man's forearm, was carved into a ball the size of a fist. The ball of the club was perfectly round except for one sharp point, carved like a tooth, on the striking face of the club. As was the custom, Two Ideas had named his club. He called it *Onawi':ra,* The Tooth. A club like that could crack open a man's head as easily as a squirrel's tooth could break an acorn.

As Two Ideas came close to the four young men, he began to spin his club, switching it from one hand to the other as he did so. His hands moved lazily, but the club made a whistling noise as it spun. Eats Like a Bear looked very sick to his stomach now, and Greasy Hair was making a small whimpering noise. Falls a Lot looked as if he could be pushed over by the smallest breeze. As before, only Grabber continued to stand up straight, but the look on his face was no longer so defiant.

Two Ideas stopped. His eyes went from one of the young men to the next. In turn, each of them looked down at the ground, even Grabber. Two Ideas nodded and started to turn away. Then, so quickly that Oh-kwa'ri hardly saw him move—even though he had sensed what was to happen next—Two Ideas spun, grabbed Eats Like a Bear by the throat, and with a piercing cry swung The Tooth down, stopping it only a finger's width from the huge young man's forehead. Eats Like a Bear put up his hands and fell down on his knees, but Two Ideas had already stepped back.

"That is what it means to go to war," Two Ideas said. Then he cradled his war club in his arm, walked back to his place, and sat down again.

The council ended soon after that. As was their way, the leaders had not told those four young men what to do and what not to do. They explained to them why their plan was not a good one, and they showed them what the consequences of their actions might be.

Big Tree stood again and looked at the four young men, who were now badly shaken.

"Hear me, all of the people," Big Tree said. "These

four young men are foolish, but they are also brave. They may still do good things for our people. In the past it has been our custom to send into exile those who do not listen, who do things that bring danger to the people. That was our custom and it is still our custom to this day. So we will continue to watch these young men, and we will look for them to do good things for all the people. *Na-ho.* I have spoken."

2

THE STRAWBERRY THANKSGIVING

Otsi:stia

Otsi:stia woke up hearing the wind. There was a story in her mind. It was not the time of the year for stories, but this one would not go away. She lifted her hand up and tried to push the story away as you would brush away a spiderweb, but the story still stayed with her.

Otsi:stia sat up and looked over at the fire, which was a few arm's lengths away from her sleeping bench. That fire always burned in their hearth. The hearth was used by her mother's family and by the family across the longhouse from them. It was one of twelve fires that were set in a line, one after another, down the length of the big lodge, each with its smoke hole in the roof four times the height of a tall man above them.

Otsi:stia pulled the warm bear robe closer around

her. This is *not* the right season for storytelling, she told herself. But this story was caught in her mind. She looked over toward the bed where her parents slept on the inner wall of their family's living place within the great longhouse.

Beds lined the two sides of the longhouse. They were used as benches for people to sit on during the day. All the people could partition off their own sleeping places and use the area under each bench bed for storing their most private possessions.

There were five beds in their family's compartment. The largest one was where Otsi:stia's parents slept. The smallest, just at the foot of her parents, was the bed her younger brother and sister shared. Otsi:stia's bed and Ohkwa'ri's were across from each other by the side walls of the partitions that marked off their space from the families on either side.

The last of the beds was at the head of Ohkwa'ri's. Only a bit larger than the one in which their little brother and sister slept, it belonged to their grandparents. It was the closest to the fire; the old people needed the warmth.

"Ohkwa'ri," Osti:stia whispered. He did not answer. No one else in her family was awake.

Otsi:stia looked up toward the smoke hole in the roof above their fire. When it rained hard, a large piece of bark could be pulled over that smoke hole, but tonight was cool and clear. She could not see the face of Grandmother Moon, but the stars that showed themselves against the blackness of the sky told her that it was still far from the time for the sun to rise.

She leaned out so that she could see down the long central walkway in the middle of the building. There were fifty families in this longhouse, but no one else except for Otsi:stia seemed to be awake. Even old man Rabbit Feet, who sometimes sat up all night by the hearth three fires down, was nowhere to be seen. The story, however, was very much awake in her mind and it would not go away. So Otsi:stia tried to turn her mind to other things.

She closed her eyes and listened. She heard the sounds of people breathing, some snoring in their sleep: her grandparents and parents, her twin, her younger sister and brother. She listened further and heard again the soft sound of the warm wind moving above the smoke hole. It was the wind that brought the first strawberries. And as she thought that, the story came back to her again. Quickly she turned her mind to other things.

This longhouse, she thought, is the longhouse of the Bear Clan. Of course, there are not only members of the Bear Clan here, although most of the two hundred people who live in the great longhouse are of the Bear Clan. There are people living in the longhouse who belong to the clans of the Turtle and the Wolf, the two other clans of our Flint Nation. But in this village the other clans are far outnumbered by the Bears. And it is my grandmother, She Opens the

Sky, who is the Clan Mother in charge of the great longhouse. It is my grandmother who is the head of the Bear Clan.

Otsi:stia thought of how it had always been that way. She thought of how their village, Kanatsiohareke, The Place of the Clean Pot, was also known to everyone as The Village of the Bears. There were two other large villages of the Flint Nation, each half a day's walk from the other, here in the beautiful valley near their river. Each belonged to one of the other clans: White Flint Village, where Ohkwa'ri's good friend Atiron lived, was the village of the Wolf Clan. Big Falls Village, where the three clans would meet when there were problems for the leaders to discuss, was the village of the Turtle Clan. And each of those villages was headed by a wise old woman—almost as wise as Otsi:stia's grandmother, She Opens the Sky. Otsi:stia thought of all this, but even as she thought it that story crept back into her mind.

Otsi:stia rolled to one side and considered the things her grandmother and mother had taught her about all the responsibilities held by the women.

We are the ones who carry life. We are the ones who care for the earth and for the Three Sisters—the corn and beans and squash that sustain us. We are the ones who keep the families together. We are the ones who pass on to our children their clan, for a child always belongs to the clan of his or her mother. We are the ones who must always watch what our boy children and our young men do so that when the time comes to choose the male leaders, as the women of our people have always done, we will choose men who are unselfish, men who have calm minds and courage, men who have great love for the people.

Those were good thoughts to have in her mind, the kind of thoughts a Clan Mother would have in her mind. But still that story would not go away. It was the story of the little boy who helped the *Iakotinen-ioia'ks*, The Little Stone-Throwing People. As a result, they took him in their magical canoe to their caves in the cliffs along the river. There they gave him many gifts to help his people. The best gift they gave was the gift of strawberries, a sweet fruit that the Flint People had never seen before. But when that boy returned to his village, even though he thought he had only been gone for a few days, he found that he was now a tall, fully grown man. Many years had passed. Everyone he knew had grown old and died.

I am thinking of this story, Otsi:stia said to herself, sitting up again and looking out at the fire, because I am worried about Ohkwa'ri. I saw the angry way Grabber stared at him after the council meeting was done. My brother is brave, but he is still a little boy compared to Grabber and his friends. That is why I am thinking of this story. I am afraid that something will happen to my brother and I will never see him again.

When Otsi:stia woke, she was still feeling tired and worried. She ate in silence, and then went with her family to join the rest of the village for the beginning of the thanksgiving.

The first to speak was their Senior Uncle, Big Tree.

"And now again this season has returned. It is to me that this matter has been given to make this speech. From my side of the council fire this speech will be brought out, this speech which is all of our good thoughts bundled together. Have patience with me, for I will do the best I can in speaking these words, even though I may not be strong enough to carry them well."

Big Tree paused and looked around at the many people who had gathered to thank the strawberries. It was early in the morning, and now that the sun had risen, time for things to begin. Big Tree was one of the best speakers in the village, but it was always the custom for the best speakers to apologize for their words. A good speaker was always modest about his ability to say things well, and a great speaker was the most modest of all.

"The one who dwells in the sky, the one who is *Shonkwaiatison,* our Creator, did this. Our Creator said, 'I will make for myself some people. On the earth they will move about.' And so it was done, and so it is to this day that we are still moving about. Then our Creator gave us what we are to do as we go along. Our Creator decided, 'This is how it will begin. They will thank me. They will begin to thank me in their thoughts. Then, when they meet each other as they move about on the earth, they will have the Thanksgiving Address. When they gather for ceremonies, they will be grateful that so many are happy. They will be contented that their minds are brought together.'

"That is what our Creator decided, and now today the time has come once more for us to bring our minds together."

Again Big Tree paused. As he did so, Otsi:stia noticed out of the corner of her eye someone stirring on the other side of the circle where the clans of the Wolf and Turtle were seated. Without moving her head, she glanced over. It was Grabber. The tall, angry-faced young man, who was a member of the Wolf Clan, was leaning over to talk with his friends. Clearly their minds were not joining together to give thanks with everyone else. Grabber looked over toward Ohkwa'ri and glared. Ohkwa'ri turned his head back to look toward his sister for reassurance.

Big Tree began to speak again. He spoke of the Earth, our Mother, and gave thanks to her. He spoke of the flowing water and the grasses. Then he came to the strawberries.

"When the wind again is warm, the people will see the new fruit hanging. It will be the first fruit they see, these strawberries. The people will see how our Creator has given them the hanging fruits, one after another each year, and the first of them all will be the strawberries. So the people will gather together to thank the Creator when they taste once again those first new fruits."

Otsi:stia always enjoyed hearing those words, but she was happy this morning when they were concluded. Now the social dances would begin. Otsi:stia had always loved them, and she thought that perhaps when she danced, her worries and that story, which would not stop telling itself to her, would go away.

The singers came out and sat on the logs set in a circle around the big outside fire pit. They began to beat the small handheld water drums and play the rattles. The leader began to sing, choosing those songs that made people want to move their feet together. Soon people were shuffling their feet, dancing to show their happiness and thanks, their backs straight as they moved. Otsi:stia joined them. From a clear sky Elder Brother, the Sun, looked down in approval.

As Otsi:stia danced, however, it seemed as if that story was dancing with her. She tried to clear her mind by thinking of all the thanksgivings that were part of each year's round in the village.

I will think first, she said to herself, of the other festivals before the Thanks to the Strawberries. The first of the new year is the great Midwinter Ceremony. Then comes the Thanks to the Maple Festival. Then there is the Thunder Dance to herald the return of those loud-voiced sky beings who are the friends of the people and bring the rain to nurture and cleanse the earth. There is the Moon Dance, giving thanks to our grandmother who watches over the night skies.

She found her feet moving more lightly now and she felt less tired. Her mother was dancing next to her and her grandmother was just in front of her. She felt that she was linked to the strength of the older women as they moved together to the heartbeat rhythm of the water drum. The story that she had not been able to forget was moving away from her. It was growing smaller, like a dancer who reaches the other side of the circle and then, instead of turning and coming back, leaves the dance. Perhaps it was the dancing or perhaps it was her good thoughts about the festivals to thank the Creator. She continued to list them in her mind.

Next, she thought, after the Thanks to the Strawberries, there is the Planting Ceremony. Later in the summer there is the Bean Dance, the festival to thank the Green Corn, and the Harvest Dance to mark the end of the summer. Then once again there is a Moon Dance to thank our Grandmother Moon, and last of all, in the season when the leaves fall, the End of the Seasons Ceremony, marking the conclusion of another cycle of seasons. Our people were given so many gifts, it is only right that we have so many special gatherings to give our thanks.

Otsi:stia laughed. Her grandmother, She Opens the

Sky, heard her laugh and turned with a smile to look down at her, reaching out her hand. Then, holding hands with her grandmother, Otsi:stia continued to dance, part of the ancient women's circle of blessing and thanks.

3

A MAN'S CUP

Ohkwa'ri and Otsi:stia

When Ohkwa'ri came that evening to sit by the central hearth in the Turtle Clan's section of the big longhouse, his uncle suspected that his nephew had something important to ask. So Big Tree continued to work in silence, giving his nephew plenty of time to collect his thoughts. It was fully dark outside now, and Grandmother Moon was looking down through the smoke hole overhead.

Big Tree picked up a burning coal from the fire with his fingers, lifted it unhurriedly, and dropped it into the wooden cup that he was making from a piece of hard maple. He had been working on that cup for two moons and it was almost finished.

Ohkwa'ri watched carefully. He remembered two winters ago when he tried to pick up a coal as his uncle did, but only succeeded in blistering his fingertips. Big Tree's fingers were tougher than Ohkwa'ri's, the callouses on them so thick that the glowing coal did not burn them.

It will be many seasons, Ohkwa'ri thought, before I can do the things that my uncle can do.

Big Tree placed the glowing coal into the bowl of the cup and nodded to his nephew. Ohkwa'ri leaned forward. This job was one that he could do now. He could help his uncle finish hollowing the bowl by blowing on the coal through the thin hollow branch of a sumac. Ohkwa'ri blew and the coal burned with a sound like that of a tiny storm wind, reddening the blackened wood, burning the hollow deeper. He moved the sumac branch as he blew steadily, puffing his cheeks in and out as he blew, making sure that the coal moved around the bowl evenly to make the inner shape of the cup just right. His uncle raised a hand and Ohkwa'ri stopped blowing. The coal, which had been the size of the end of his thumb, was now a tiny spark. Big Tree took his sharp-edged scraping stone and used it to clean out the bowl.

"This is good," his uncle said. "Now I only have to smooth the inside and this cup will be ready to use."

He held it up and both he and Ohkwa'ri admired it. The finely detailed handle was the long head of a bear. Big Tree had used his sharp flint knife to finish off the details of the bear's head at the front of the cup, even making marks that looked like the fur of the bear. Then he had blackened it in the fire to harden and darken it and make it look even more like a bear.

"Who will be the owner of this cup, my uncle?" Ohkwa'ri asked.

"A man who needs it," his uncle replied with a smile.

Ohkwa'ri nodded. Every man owned a cup such as that, usually with some design on it which indicated his clan. Your cup, which would be hung from your belt, could be used for dipping up drinking water when you were in the forest.

Dipping water with a cup was a wise idea, for you could remain watchful and alert while doing this. If you had to lean down and drink with your mouth from the spring or the stream, an enemy or a dangerous animal could creep up unseen. You also could thrust the cup deep under the surface where the water was cleaner and colder. Then, when you were back in the longhouse, you could use your cup to dip soup from the pot when the food was ready and your hunger told you to eat.

Ohkwa'ri already had a cup of his own, a small one made of soft basswood that hung on his belt. But that cup was plain and chipped and it was not well carved. It was a boy's cup. It was useful, but it was better to have something that was useful and beautiful.

Ohkwa'ri put the sumac blowpipe back on the shelf above his uncle's bed. Like all things that would be useful to more than one person, it was kept in plain sight. That way, if anyone in the village had need of it they could simply take it and return it when they were done. Truly personal things—like Ohkwa'ri's stone with its two beautiful crystals—were kept out of sight in the bark boxes under everyone's beds. No one would ever look under another person's bed.

Ohkwa'ri came and sat back down by his uncle, who continued to work on smoothing the inside of the cup.

"Uncle," Ohkwa'ri said, "I think it is time for me to build a lodge."

Big Tree continued to work on the cup without saying anything in response.

"I do not mean that I think it is time for me to move away from my mother's hearth," Ohkwa'ri said. "I know that it is still two or three winters before it will be time for me to do that, to go and live on my own. But I think that it would be good for me to make a little lodge and sleep in it some nights. It would be a good way to learn, a good way to make myself tougher and stronger."

Ohkwa'ri's words were true. In another few winters he would be expected to move out of the longhouse, to no longer live near his mother. Then he would need to know how to care for himself. Every boy came to this time in his life when he was expected to go through a whole year of the hard training needed to be accepted fully as a man. He would find a place outside the village and build his own lodge, sleeping there every night. Although he could still return to the big longhouse and take meals with his family, he would truly be responsible for himself.

Ohkwa'ri waited and still his uncle said nothing. Then Ohkwa'ri realized why his uncle was silent. Ohkwa'ri had only been telling his uncle what he hoped to do. He had not yet asked a single question of his uncle or made it clear that he wanted his uncle's advice.

"My uncle," Ohkwa'ri said slowly, "would you tell me what you think of my idea?"

Big Tree looked up from his work. There was a smile on his face as if he were trying not to laugh.

"My nephew," he said, "yesterday you spoke bravely in the council circle. But now you have made Grabber and his friends think you are their enemy. If you make a little lodge somewhere away from the village, they might find you there and attack you. Is that not true?"

Ohkwa'ri tried to think of the right words to say. Otsi:stia was always telling him that he spoke and acted too quickly. He took a deep breath.

"My uncle," Ohkwa'ri said, "that may be true, even though I am not their enemy. So I think it is even more important now for me to do things to become tougher and stronger. As far as Grabber and the others are concerned . . ." Ohkwa'ri paused. "I am sorry if they hate me, but I will not run away from them. A bear doesn't run away like a rabbit. Is that not true?"

Big Tree laughed. Ohkwa'ri could tell that he was

not laughing at him, for it was the sort of laugh he had heard from his uncle when Big Tree found his favorite food in the pot or when something good was said to him. Big Tree was surely thinking of how right the name of Ohkwa'ri, which meant "Bear," was for his nephew.

"Ohkwa'ri," Big Tree said, "it is true, indeed. I agree that it is a good idea for you to build a small lodge." He leaned forward and placed the finished cup into Ohkwa'ri's hands. "As I said, a man needs this cup. So, my nephew, this cup is yours."

Ohkwa'ri held the cup in both hands. It was the most beautiful thing that he had ever been given. He did not know what to say.

Big Tree turned his head and thrust out his lips toward the other end of the big longhouse. "Now go and get your twin sister. I have something I want to share with both of you."

Otsi:stia looked up as her brother came running down the central corridor of the longhouse. He had looked troubled when he rose after eating and walked in the direction of the Turtle Clan section, where their uncle Big Tree lived with his wife's family. But the look on Ohkwa'ri's face was very different now, excited and triumphant.

"Look," he said, thrusting out his hands toward his sister so suddenly that he almost tripped and fell into the fire. Otsi:stia steadied him by grabbing his elbow. Then she saw what he held.

"Aaah!" Otsi:stia breathed. The cup was so perfectly carved that she knew only Big Tree could have made it. Everyone in their village admired Big Tree's ability to carve things from wood. He was not only the maker of cups like this one. He was also the carver of the two man-high poles set up outside the east and west approaches to their village along the river, the *Te-uge-ga Ga-hun-da,* The River at the Forks. Big Tree's clever hands carved the powerful wooden faces that spoke with the voices of the great beings during ceremonies. To have something made by Big Tree was to have something truly wonderful.

"Ourunclegavethistome," Ohkwa'ri said, speaking so fast that it all came out as one word. "He . . ." Ohkwa'ri saw the look on his sister's face and took a deep breath before she could tell him to do so, " . . . wants-us-to-come-back-to-their-hearth. He has something to share with us. *Hanio!* Come on!"

Otsi:stia stood up. She felt excited, but she was determined to set a good example for her headstrong brother. "That is good," she said. "Let us *walk* over to his hearth together."

Big Tree was still sitting by the fire, waiting for them. They sat down next to him as he put another piece of peeled elm log into the fire and then stirred the coals with a long stick.

"This is not the season to tell stories," Big Tree began.

Otsi:stia had begun rebraiding her long hair as soon as she sat down. Those words of her uncle's startled her so much that she yanked hard, undoing the braid. Had her uncle heard her thinking about stories? She looked up and saw that his eyes were not on her but on the fire.

"As you know, those ancient stories are only meant to be told when the days are short and the nights are long. The *Iakotinenioia'ks,* The Little Stone-Throwing People, are the guardians of those stories, and if they hear them being told in the spring or the summer, they may throw a rock or turn themselves into bees and come and sting the lips of the one who is telling that story."

"Henh!" said Ohkwa'ri, voicing his agreement. Otsi:stia elbowed him in the ribs.

"There are other kinds of stories, though," Big Tree said. "There are the stories of how our Great League was founded, and the stories of how our people traveled far to come to this land. Such stories, such histories of our people can be told in any season. So I have chosen to tell you this one tonight."

"Henh," said Ohkwa'ri, leaning away from his sister as he said it so she could not elbow him again. But this time, to his surprise, Otsi:stia also added a loud *"Henh!"* of her own.

"Long ago," Big Tree said, looking down at the Mother Earth as he spoke—as if asking her to listen and confirm the truth of his words—"our people lived far to the west. There we were brothers with the Wolf People, and we lived among the great mounds of earth by the big river, *Ka-hu-ah'-go Ga-hun-da*. The grass was tall there, and there were herds of buffalo. We were happy there with our brothers, but as things happen sometimes, there was disagreement.

"In those days, we remembered the original instructions of our Creator. The instructions were simple in those days. All that we had to do was remember to be thankful. So every morning we would say the great prayer of thanksgiving, remembering to thank everything around us. We thanked our Mother, the Earth, we thanked the plants and animals, we thanked the Thunder Beings, the Sun and Moon and Stars and the Creator. You know this Thanksgiving, for we still speak that prayer.

"People did not fight with each other back then. We were all of one family. So, because there was strong disagreement, the only thing we could do was to move away. It was decided then that we who disagreed would leave there and travel toward the sunrise. We traveled a long, long time. We came to the mountains and there were two trails. One led southeast, one led northeast. Again there was disagreement. Half of the people took the trail to the southeast. They live now far to the south of us, they are the Oyatageronon people."

Big Tree paused, and this time both Otsi:stia and Ohkwa'ri spoke as one the word that meant both "yes" and that they were listening.

"Henh!"

Big Tree continued his story.

"The journey was a long one and sometimes it was hard along the way. They met other nations of people. Most were friendly, but some were worried that our people would settle in their hunting grounds, and so they did not allow us to make camp for more than a few moons before they urged us to go farther toward the sunrise. There were times when our people went hungry and other times when the hunters had to protect them from big dangerous animals that we had never seen when we lived on the plains near the great river. Now the forest grew thick and the trees were bigger and taller than any trees we had ever seen before. We continued on through that great forest."

Once again Big Tree stopped.

"Henh," said Ohkwa'ri and Otsi:stia.

Big Tree nodded. "As our people traveled," he said, "still more bands decided to go in other directions. Those who went north, beyond the big inland seas of sweet water, became the Huron. But we continued on along the shores of the lakes until we came to a river that flowed from below the big falls we call *Ne-ah-gah*. It flowed up toward the winter land and toward the sunrise. That river led into another lake, the one we call *Ska-no'-dar-io*, The Beautiful Lake. Again we followed its shore until we came to a great river running swiftly. It was the *Ga-na-wa-ga Ga-hun-da*, The Rapid River. And after we traveled its banks for the journey of a moon, we came to a fine place to live. We knew we had found our new home."

"Henh!"

Big Tree smiled and looked at Otsi:stia. Her face was so very much like Ohkwa'ri's. She was braiding her long hair absentmindedly as she listened intently.

"It was only when our people had reached the place that would be our home that the real trouble began. There were people already living there. Those people spoke a different language, and they did not look like us. There were far more of them than there were of our people. We saw how they used the bark of the trees to season their food, and because of this we called them Porcupine People, Bark-Eating People, Anen:taks. Things did not go well between us. They tried to drive us out of their land, and we fought many battles with them until they defeated us. Then they forced us to pay tribute to them and to act like their slaves.

"Our people could not stand that. We wanted to be free. So we made canoes out of elm bark, and one night we tried to escape by going up the river. The Anen:taks soon found that we were gone and they followed us. Their birch bark canoes were much faster, and they caught up to us late the next day. It seemed as if we would be taken back as slaves. But that was when the Thunder Beings, the ones we always remembered to thank for bringing us the rain to make our crops grow, took pity on us. The Thunder Beings sent a great wind and a great storm. The canoes of the Anen:tak people were overturned by the wind and the storm and many of them drowned. Those Anen:taks who survived returned to their villages and never tried again to make slaves of our people."

Big Tree leaned back from the fire and looked at Otsi:stia and Ohkwa'ri.

"That," he said, "is usually as far as we tell this story. But there is more. Otsi:stia, tell me, what do you think happened next?"

Otsi:stia stopped braiding and rebraiding her hair. She cupped her hands together and held them up to her mouth, thinking hard. At last she nodded.

"Then we made peace with the Anen:taks and began to trade with them."

"That is right," Big Tree said. His voice was very pleased. "We did not try to make them our slaves, and we did not try to wipe them out. Although we have not always been their friends, ever since that time long ago we have tried to remain at peace with them."

Big Tree reached out his long arms, placing one big hand on Otsi:stia's shoulder and the other on Ohkwa'ri's.

"That is what we do," Big Tree said. "That is the way of the People of the Longhouse. We fight when we need to fight, but we seek to be at peace with those who make themselves our enemies. Those same Anen:tak people are the ones that Grabber and his companions planned to raid. So it was a very good thing that both of you did. That is why I have shared this story with you tonight.

"*Na-ho.* I have spoken."

4

THE NEW LODGE

Ohkwa'ri

*A*fter Ohkwa'ri crossed the river and climbed up the opposite bank, he looked back down toward his home. It was nearly hidden among the big trees in the shadow of the great hill everyone called The Big Nose. It looked like the small longhouse of sticks and pieces of bark that he had once made.

It was strange how big things grew small when one moved away from them, Ohkwa'ri thought. Their longhouse was so large that it could easily hold every family in their entire village—hundreds of people, even including those who lived in the four smaller longhouses around it. In the winter, when the smokes of the central fires in the big longhouse filled the air, you could not see from one end of it to the other. Yet from a distance it looked like something made by a child, smaller than the small lodge he was now about to make for himself.

His uncle Big Tree had explained it to him. "When you have walked far away from something, you will see it as a part of all that is around you. When it is close, it may seem bigger than anything else, but our Creator was wise and made it so that we could also see things from a distance."

Ohkwa'ri reached his hand down and lifted up the drinking cup which now hung from his belt. He had not realized when Big Tree was making it that it was meant to be his. But he understood why his uncle had given him the cup.

Ohkwa'ri let the cup drop from his hand to hang back at his side from its braided deerskin string. He stood up and looked at the saplings he had already cut to make his lodge. The day would be a long one. However, if he was going to complete even the roughest of lodges for himself before Elder Brother, the Sun, left the sky, then he would have to keep working.

He picked up the small ax again to cut one more pole from the stand of young maples. He had spoken to the largest of the maple trees, which arced over the many saplings, explaining his need to make a lodge.

"My friends," Ohkwa'ri had said, "you and your elders give us many gifts. You have just given us that sweet sap, which is our favorite drink. You know that we have thanked you for that with our ceremony of thanksgiving. You know that we always treat you with respect, for you are the chief of the trees. Now

I ask you for something else. There are so many of your young ones here that they do not have room to grow. I am going to cut just a few to make my lodge poles. I will do so in a way that gives the other young trees more light and more room."

Then he had begun to cut out the trees, cutting them very close to the ground so that no stubs would stick up to trip anyone walking here. It had not been hard to do with the small ax, for it was a very fine one. His younger uncle, Hand Talker, had made it, and everyone knew how good a craftsman he was, even better than his older brother, Big Tree. Perhaps Hand Talker was the best maker of tools in the Village of the Bears.

Ohkwa'ri hefted the ax again in his hand, feeling how good its balance was. The blade was a solid piece of stone, the shape of a hand with the fingers held close together. It was fitted tightly into the handle, which had been split to hold it and then bound above and below the stone. The stone had been pressure flaked so that it was sharp enough to cut wood, though nowhere near as sharp as the smaller flint blades that were made into knives keen enough to skin an animal. On the handle was the carved-in shape of a hand held open, palm out, Hand Talker's personal sign that he put on everything he made. Ohkwa'ri grasped the handle tightly with one hand and bent the small trunk of the sapling with the other hand so that the blade would not bounce off the sapling as he struck. Circling the trunk with a handful of careful strokes, he cut the little tree.

When he had finished trimming the small branches from the sapling, he added them to the brush pile that he had made near a tangle of blackberry stalks. Such a brush pile would be useful as shelter for small animals such as the rabbit.

Ohkwa'ri smiled as he added the branches, thinking of one of the brush piles on the other side of their village across the river. The pile was not far from the hilltop where he had dug out his cave under the slanting stone. Only two days ago as he walked up to his cave, he had seen a rabbit go into that brush pile. Moving as slowly as a stalking bobcat, he had crawled over to the pile. It took him so long that Elder Brother, the Sun, moved the width of two hands across the sky.

But it had been worth it. When he looked into the hole in the brush pile, he saw a little nest in the earth that was lined with rabbit fur. In that nest were five baby rabbits. They looked so soft that Ohkwa'ri wanted to reach in and pick them up and hold them to his cheek. But he did not touch them. He only watched for a while, breathing slowly and smiling as they moved around in their nest. Then, as quietly and slowly as he had crept close, he had backed away.

"Perhaps," Ohkwa'ri said, speaking both to himself and to the small maple trees which had sacrificed themselves to help him, "this brush pile will be the home for another family of rabbits like the ones I saw. Truly, my friends, you have given more than one gift by allowing me to cut you."

Ohkwa'ri stood back to take a careful look. He had used a small pole the length of a spear, but twice as thick, to make the holes in which he would thrust the base of each of the saplings that would make the framework of his lodge. Early that morning, back in the longhouse, he had sharpened the pole with the flint knife he carried in a sheath that hung about his neck. Then he had hardened the sharp pole by holding it in the hearth fire until it was blackened.

The holes he had pierced made a circle. There were thirteen of them, for this lodge was not going to be flat-sided and elongated like the longhouses built to hold many families. Instead, this would be a personal lodge, much like the ones used by the Anen:taks.

Ohkwa'ri squatted down on his haunches and leaned against the pole, which he still held. He let his eyes sweep out over the river below, the *Te-uge-ga Ga-hun-da*. He could see one canoe crossing there below him near the place where he had crossed in his own small elm bark canoe.

He saw this, but he also saw in his mind another, wider water and many canoes. He saw the story Big Tree had told him of how the People of the Longhouse gained their freedom from the Anen:tak people who treated them like slaves.

Ohkwa'ri shook his head. The small canoe he had

seen crossing was now out of sight. And Elder Brother, the Sun, had moved still farther up into the sky. He would have to hurry if he hoped to finish his lodge.

He moved aside the pile of elm bark shingles. He had carried them across the river in his canoe, taking three trips to do so. They were pieces which had been given him by some of the men who had been peeling elm bark to repair the big lodge.

"Ohkwa'ri," they had called to him, "come over here. Do you want these little pieces of elm bark? They are too small for us to use. You might as well have them." Then they had given him more than enough to cover the small lodge he planned to make, even some pieces that would have been large enough for them to use in their repairs.

Ohkwa'ri could tell the older men were pleased and amused by his seriousness. He wondered whether they had only decided to gather elm bark for repairs after hearing about his plan to make a lodge of his own.

Ohkwa'ri took one of the maple poles and began to thrust it into one of the holes. As he did so, he heard from behind him the sharp crack of a stick breaking, as if someone had stepped on it. He whirled around to see who had crept up on him.

A tall, happy-faced man stood there. The dry stick that he had just snapped was held in his hand. It was Ohkwa'ri's younger uncle, Hand Talker.

Hand Talker dropped the stick and held out his hand to tap the pole that Ohkwa'ri had been placing in the ground. He made a motion, as if lifting the pole up. Ohkwa'ri pulled the pole out of the ground.

Hand Talker made another motion, as if drawing something toward himself.

Ohkwa'ri understood. He handed the lodge pole to his uncle.

Hand Talker smiled at him and then thrust the pole under the stub of his left arm. He had lost that arm in the same fall which hurt his throat so badly that his voice had been broken. He rested the slender tip of the pole on the ground and pulled his knife out of his belt sheath. Then, with careful strokes away from himself, he began to peel the bark from the part of the pole that would go into the ground.

Ohkwa'ri breathed in quickly. He felt angry at himself for being so foolish as to forget that an unpeeled pole set into the ground will rot quickly. Then he shook his head and smiled as his younger uncle had smiled. Hand Talker had not intended to make him feel foolish. Hand Talker had only wanted to help, and he had done so in the friendly way that made everyone admire him. Ohkwa'ri picked up a pole himself, took out his own knife, and began to peel away the bark as his uncle was doing. The bark was loose, for the trees were still wet with the sap of spring, and he had only to make a few cuts down the pole to start freeing the bark. After that he could pull it free with his fingers.

Even with only one hand his uncle was faster than he was. In the time it took Ohkwa'ri to peel three poles, his uncle had done all of the others.

It is surely true, Ohkwa'ri thought, as my mother told me. When a man or a woman has something taken from them, the Creator gives them something in return.

It had only been after his accident, falling from the cliffs where he had climbed to look into a nest of young eagles, that Hand Talker had turned into the finest toolmaker in their village. He was able to do just about anything anyone else could, except use a bow and arrow. He could even paddle a canoe with one arm. It was Hand Talker's canoe that Ohkwa'ri had seen crossing the river below him. And even without a speaking voice Hand Talker was always able to make people understand him well with the gestures of his one hand.

Once again Ohkwa'ri began to put the poles into the earth, moving around in a circle as he did so until all of the poles were firmly set. Hand Talker leaned against a tree as his nephew worked, nodding now and then in approval.

It was not until Ohkwa'ri began to bend two poles together, one from each side of the circle, so that he could tie their overlapping ends to make the first part of the roof arch, that he looked over to his uncle for help. Ohkwa'ri said nothing. He did not need to speak. Hand Talker understood immediately, came close, and reached out his hand to hold the ends of the bent poles together while his nephew lashed them firmly. Ohkwa'ri used the thin strips of inner bark he had peeled from a basswood tree and then softened by running them back and forth over a smooth rock. Such basswood strings were almost as supple as deerskin and much stronger.

As Ohkwa'ri bent and tied other pairs of poles, he thought of how little he said aloud when his uncle Hand Talker was alone with him. It was as if they could communicate better without words, as if they could hear more clearly what was in each other's mind.

Ohkwa'ri found himself remembering something his other grandmother, Walks Quietly, once said to him. He had been playing the spear and hoop game with a group of children of his age. He was so excited that he was running and shouting as he played.

"Throw it now," he had shouted, "hit it before it stops rolling."

Suddenly he had run right into his grandmother. But even though he was big for his age and Walks Quietly was only a little taller than he was, he bounced off her as if he had run into a tree. She had seen him coming toward her and braced herself by bending her knees and putting one foot back behind her.

"Ohhhkwaa'ri," she had said then, drawing his name out in a teasing way as he peered up at her with a dazed look on his face, "do you know why the Creator made us with two eyes and only one mouth?"

"No, Grandmother," Ohkwa'ri had answered.

"It is because we always need to look twice as much as we talk. Then we will be less likely to run into things."

Ohkwa'ri tied the last of the poles. Carefully crisscrossed together at the top, they now made a shape like the shell of a turtle. Then, again with his uncle Hand Talker's help, Ohkwa'ri tied on the thinner saplings that went around the lodge, holding it more firmly together and making rings on which he could fasten the elm bark shingles. He left open the doorway, remembering how he had tried to make such a lodge two winters before and then realized that he had not left an opening for a door. This doorway faced downriver, the direction of the sunrise.

When they had tied the last of the sapling rings in place, Hand Talker raised his hand, turned, and went back down the path to the river. He knew that his nephew would be able to do the rest of the work of lodge-building without his help.

Ohkwa'ri touched his own hand to his heart and swung it out toward his uncle. Even though his back was turned, he was certain that Hand Talker knew he was saying thank you, giving his heart in gratitude to his uncle for the guidance he had been given.

Hand Talker could never become one of the Good Men, the *Roia:ne*. Even if his older brother should die, or through misdeeds have the horns of his office taken from him by his Clan Mother, Ohkwa'ri's younger uncle could never assume the name and the position of Shoskoharo'wane, The Big Tree. A Good Man had to speak with great eloquence at the councils, and Hand Talker's silent tongue prevented him from being able to do that. Yet as Ohkwa'ri watched his uncle disappear down the slope, he knew that Hand Talker was happy being who he was and no one else. In his own way Hand Talker too was one who always spoke for peace.

5

STRAWBERRIES

Otsi:stia

Otsi:stia put one of the strawberries into her mouth. It was warm from the sun that shone down in such a friendly way on the women who were spread out through the meadow near the river. Nothing tasted as sweet as these first strawberries, not even the syrup made from the maple tree. She held up another strawberry between her fingers. It was perfectly ripe on all sides. Her grandmother had explained to her that the Little People, the Jungies, took special care of the strawberries. When no humans were around to watch, the Jungies would go through the fields, turning the strawberries so that they would ripen evenly.

Otsi:stia remembered walking to the strawberry fields this morning. Her path had taken her through the edge of woods that came down like an arm around the sunrise side of their village. There were many medicine plants growing there. Otsi:stia liked to walk past them, identifying them and reminding herself again of their healing uses. The women of the Bear Clan were known to be the best healers among all of the Clans of the Longhouse People, and it was also said that of the Five Nations, the Bear Clan women of her Flint Nation were the best of all.

Otsi:stia had noticed that the cradleboard flower was now in bloom. It looked much like a pale little person nestled in a propped-up cradleboard. She had bent down and lifted up the single green petal decorated with dark stripes that hung over the little one inside the flower.

"Little One in your cradleboard," she had sung softly, "your mother has hung you here from a tree limb. Now as the wind comes, your cradleboard sways. Sleep, little one, sleep."

Then she had stood and recited what she had heard her mother say about the way to use this medicine. "Cradleboard root. Cradleboard root. Boil it and the steam will help sore eyes."

Remembering the medicine plants as she put the red strawberries into her basket, Otsi:stia thought of the story of the coming of medicines.

Surely it is all right to think about this story, even if it is not the season to tell it, she said to herself. Then she began to tell in her mind the story of how medicines were given to the women of the Bear Clan.

Long ago, the story went, *Shonkwaiatison,* the Creator, decided to come down to the Earth to see how the people were doing, to see if they remembered his teachings. Those original teachings were simple ones. They said that human beings should be kind to each other, be thankful, and show respect for all things. So he came down in the shape of a great shooting star. Many people saw it blaze across the sky, but no one saw it strike the Earth. And no one saw that where it struck the Earth, a shabbily dressed old man now stood. His leggings were covered with burrs, and his moccasins were worn so thin that they had holes in them. His loincloth was torn and his shirt was stained. His white hair was tangled and dirty.

Then the old man, who was the Creator in disguise, went to a village of the People of the Longhouse. It was a village of the Turtle Clan. He knew this when he saw a turtle shell above the door of the main longhouse. But when he asked for help, the Clan Mother turned him away because he was dirty and sick.

The old man left that village and began to walk again, leaning on a stick. The next village was a village of the Wolf Clan, for there was the carved head of a wolf hung over the door of the main longhouse. There too he was driven away by the Clan Mother. On and on the old man went, from one village to another, until he had visited every clan but one. He was rejected by the Eel Clan, the Snipe, the Deer and the Beaver and the Hawk.

At last, feeling sad because his people had forgotten his original teachings, he came to a village where a bear paw was carved over the door of the longhouse. There, even before he reached the door, the Clan Mother came out and welcomed him, calling him "Grandfather." She gave him food and clean clothes and she combed his hair. Then she gave him the best bed in the longhouse.

Otsi:stia smiled as she thought of that story. She looked over toward the edge of the strawberry fields where the woods began. A little patch of bloodroot flowers still bloomed here in the cool of the forest, looking like a patch of leftover snow. Their sap was good to use as a dressing for cuts and wounds. That was why it was the color of blood, to remind people of how the flowers could be used to help.

She thought again of how that long-ago Bear Clan's Clan Mother had done such a good job of taking care of the weak old man who was the Creator in disguise.

If I found an old man who was sick and in need of help, I would be certain to help him, she thought. I would never turn him away.

It was hard to believe that the other Clan Mothers had forgotten so much of the original teachings. But because the people of the Bear Clan had remembered, they were given the gift of knowing the healing plants. For that old man, who was the Creator in disguise, became sick—not once, but many times. Each time he taught the Bear Clan's Clan Mother what plants to gather and how to use them to cure his sickness. That was how the Creator gave the knowledge of healing to the Bear Clan.

"And that is why, to this day," Otsi:stia said to the bloodroot plants, "we are the best doctors of all the clans."

Her grandmother told them so many good stories. Those stories always had good lessons attached to them, and although some of the boys and girls were only interested in the excitement and the mystery of the tales, Otsi:stia always tried to figure out what could be learned from them. Stories were wonderful and powerful, and Otsi:stia herself had already decided that when she was as old as She Opens the Sky, she would tell stories to the little children in that very same way. She would tell the stories about the Little People, the stories about how the world was made on the back of the great turtle and how the birds and animals taught things to the real human beings. Then Otsi:stia remembered something else and it troubled her.

She turned to her mother, Herons Flying. Her mother was as tall and graceful as the great blue birds which had flown low over the birthing lodge on the day she was born. Those herons were the first thing the midwife saw after the little girl drew her first breath, and so the child was named for them.

"My mother," Otsi:stia said, "I have a question."

"My daughter," Herons Flying said in a low, grave voice, "I already have an answer for you. You cannot put as many strawberries into your mouth as you can fit into your berry basket."

"No," Otsi:stia said, wiping her mouth, "that is not my question. I am not joking, Mother."

"My daughter," Herons Flying said, putting her own, much fuller strawberry basket aside and turning to look at her serious-faced daughter, "I will stop teasing. Ask me your question."

"Actually, I have two questions, my mother."

Herons Flying nodded her head. It was usually this way with her twin children. Their younger sister and brother were also inquisitive ones, but usually they asked only one question at a time. When Otsi:stia or Ohkwa'ri started asking questions, it made the one being asked—usually their mother—feel as if she had just come back from a scouting mission and was reporting to the elders. "Only two questions, my daughter?" Herons Flying said.

"First of all, it is true that we are not to tell the old stories in the time between the last frost and the first frost. Is that not so?"

"That is true, my daughter. The time for storytelling comes when the leaves change color, and it lasts through the moons of long nights until it is time once more for us to start planting our crops. We do not tell those stories in the spring and the summer."

"Is it because the Little People are listening to us

that we don't tell the stories in the spring and the summer?"

"That is your second question, my daughter," Herons Flying said. "And I will answer it as best I can. I was told by your grandmother and your grandfather and other wise elders that the Little People are the ones who take care of many things in the world around us. Some of them carry the dew in little cups to water the corn and beans and squash. Others help take care of the animal and bird people. They guard the entrances to the caves that go deep under the earth, keeping the terrible monsters that live there from escaping to harm us. And some of the Little People listen to us when we gather together. Maybe that is because they know we have special dances to honor them, and they are waiting to hear if we are going to play those songs. But if they hear someone start to tell a story during the wrong season, then maybe that Little Person will turn into a bee and fly in and sting the one telling the story on the lip. Like this bee here, perhaps."

Herons Flying reached out a hand to gently stroke the back of a bumblebee that was working hard on a flower next to them.

Otsi:stia was silent for a few breaths. Herons Flying did not turn back to her berry picking, though. She knew that look on her daughter's face.

"My mother, I have another question," Otsi:stia said at last.

"Only one more?" said Herons Flying.

"I understand that we should not tell the old stories in the spring and the summer. We should not tell those stories now. But what about thinking about the stories now? I can't stop thinking about them. Things happen and they make me think of one or another of those old stories. And you have told me that the Little People can hear what we are thinking. They know if we have good thoughts or bad thoughts. Just as the medicine plants in the forest know if our thoughts are good when we go to gather them and will hide if we are thinking the wrong things."

Otsi:stia paused to take a breath. Her face was very serious.

"My daughter," Herons Flying said, "it is all right to think of the stories at any time. Those stories are told to you so that they will always be with you. Thinking of them is not the same as telling them aloud."

Otsi:stia smiled. "You are certain, my mother?" she said.

"I am certain," said Herons Flying. "Now let us see which of us can fill our baskets with the most straw-berries before either of us says another thing."

Otsi:stia's hands were slender and quick as they darted back and forth like hummingbirds among the berry plants. Her basket filled quickly, though her mind was not completely on the strawberries she was gathering. Her mind was thinking stories. Each thing she saw brought another story and its lesson to mind. The berries she picked made her think of the tale of the little boy who shared the game he caught with the Little People. In return, those Little People showed him many plants that would be useful for his people—including the strawberries.

A crow flew overhead, and she thought of the story of how corn was first brought to the people by the crows. So every year they would come to tell the people it was time for the corn planting to begin. In return, the people would always leave some corn in the fields for the crows to harvest.

A late-blooming white bloodroot flower bowed its head to her as the wind swayed it. Otsi:stia thought of the tale of Old Man Winter and Young Man Spring. Winter lived in a cold lodge with a fire made of ice. He thought that he would keep the world frozen forever. But when Young Man Spring came to visit the old man, Winter's lodge melted away. Where his cold fire had been, there was left a circle of white flowers.

Everything she saw had a story connected to it, and being able to think of those stories at any time made her feel very happy. She wanted to share her happiness with her friends, especially Ohkwa'ri, her brother. She knew that he had been wanting to ask that same question about whether or not it was wrong to think of the stories when it was not the storytelling seasons. But, as was usually the case, she had been the first one to ask. And now she would be able to tell him.

Otsi:stia looked across the river toward the open meadow. She put one hand up to shade her eyes, and she could see a little smoke rising from a fire. It had to be Ohkwa'ri's fire. She knew that today was the day he was going to try to make a lodge all by himself. She worried a little about him. He was still quite young to do something such as that. Although they were twins, she had been born a few heartbeats before her brother. So she was the older one. And as the older, she had to be more responsible.

Some day, Otsi:stia thought, I might live long enough to be a Clan Mother like She Opens the Sky.

Perhaps by then Ohkwa'ri would be a *Roia:ne*, be the one carrying the name of Big Tree. Then, as Clan Mother, it would be Otsi:stia's responsibility to tell him the decisions made by the women and help him to represent the people with honor and care. But if that day was going to come, Ohkwa'ri was going to have to learn to be less reckless.

Otsi:stia shook her head as she thought about her brother building his little lodge. It was not safe for him to be alone and away from the village now. She had seen the way that Grabber and his friends had looked at him during the Strawberry Festival.

Why did our uncle agree that it was a good idea for him to build a lodge of his own now? she thought, and then sighed.

Herons Flying, picking berries a few arm's lengths away, noticed that sigh and that familiar head shake out of the corner of her eye. She smiled, knowing that her daughter was once again playing the role of much wiser older sister in her thoughts.

"Mother?" Otsi:stia said.

"Yes, my daughter. Do you have yet another question?"

"No," Otsi:stia said. "It is just that I have been thinking about Ohkwa'ri. Will he be safe tonight?"

"He will not be any safer if you worry about him, my daughter."

Otsi:stia said nothing. But as she returned to her berry picking, she sighed and shook her head once more.

"Mother."

"Yes, Otsi:stia."

"I understand that Ohkwa'ri wishes to be alone tonight. He does not wish to be disturbed. But it seems to me that it would not disturb him if I were to leave some berries by the trail at the base of the hill. He will be hungry when he comes down from his lodge, and he would like some of those berries."

"Yes, my daughter. I am sure that Ohkwa'ri would like that."

As Otsi:stia carried her basket of berries toward the river, she thought about those four young men who were so angry at her brother. It was hard to understand why some became like Grabber and his friends. They had not been treated badly by their elders. It was true that Grabber's father was gone, but he had good grandparents. Neither he nor Eats Like a Bear nor Greasy Hair nor Falls a Lot had ever been mistreated as far as Otsi:stia knew.

Sometimes people became confused when they were badly treated or when their dreams were not listened to so that they could understand the deep wishes within their spirits. But Otsi:stia was fairly certain that was not the case with those four young men. During the Midwinter Festival they had been listened to when they spoke about their dreams. All four of them had been treated well and listened to. They had been given good names at birth. But those names were hardly ever spoken because of the unfortunate nicknames they had earned that suited each of them so well.

Otsi:stia was thinking so hard that at first she did not notice she was being followed. It was only when she reached the trail which led down to the river crossing that she heard the first sound of someone's feet tripping over something in the thick brush to the side of the trail.

Falls a Lot, Otsi:stia thought. She stopped and bent down, pretending that she had to retie the lacing on one of her moccasins. She listened. She could hear them now. There was more than one person trailing her. They were less than a spear's throw away from her in the tangle of grapevines and willow and alder that grew along the riverbank. She could hear one person's heavy breathing. That is Eats Like a Bear, she thought.

Otsi:stia understood why they were trailing her. They did not know where Ohkwa'ri had gone. They hoped that she would lead them to her brother. And if she had not heard the sound of one clumsy person—surely Falls a Lot—making noise, she would have done just that. Otsi:stia felt angry, but she put a smile on her face as she stood back up.

"Ah, my brother," she said out loud, "you will enjoy these berries so much when I bring them to you." Then she began to walk as fast as she could, passing the trail that led down to the river crossing and continuing on. Her smile grew even broader when she heard the sounds of someone falling as they tried to run through the brush next to her.

Otsi:stia chose her path carefully. She turned to go down the trail that led through the thickly grown blackberry bushes. She was careful to stop every now and then to look around, as if enjoying the beauty of the day. That way the two following her would not get too far behind. Each time she stopped, she heard what seemed to be muffled cries of pain. Those blackberry thorns are sharp, are they not? Otsi:stia thought. She continued walking, making a great arc that led farther away from the river.

Now the sun was beginning to go down behind the

tall hills. It was time for Otsi:stia to make her last move. She looked up the trail where it curved toward the hilltop just ahead, a hill with many loose sharp stones.

"Ohkwa'ri," she called out loudly, "it is your sister. I am climbing up to bring you some berries."

Otsi:stia ran around the curve in the trail so quickly that she knew she would be out of sight of those following her. Then, just as quickly, she stepped off the trail to hide behind the wide trunk of an ancient pine. To make sure those following her would stay on what they thought was her trail, she threw a handful of strawberries from her basket farther up the path. Then she crouched down out of sight.

Soon she heard heavy feet coming up the trail. They stopped just past the tree.

"Look," said an excited voice, "there are some berries she dropped." It was Falls a Lot.

"Give me some of them," said a deep rumbling voice. Otsi:stia covered her mouth, trying not to laugh. She knew who that was. It was no wonder that Eats Like a Bear and Falls a Lot were regarded as two of the worst hunters in the village. They were so noisy that all the animals in the forest would hear them coming from far, far away.

Soon the two young men went up the path and around the hill. Otsi:stia waited until she heard the sound of stones rattling on the hillside. Then she knew they were trying to climb to the top. She shook her head at their foolishness and then, coming out from behind the tree, headed back down the trail toward the river crossing. There would still be enough light for her to cross over and leave the berries for her brother. And this time she knew she would not be followed.

6

THE NIGHT ALONE

Ohkwa'ri

*T*he first two times during the night when Ohkwa'ri woke up, he tried to reach under what he thought was his usual bed to find the elm bark box in which he kept his stone. That stone had in it two big, beautiful crystals, each as big as a man's thumb. It was his favorite possession, and he sometimes took it out in the night to hold it above him and watch the light from their central fire flicker and reflect from its facets. He realized now that reaching for that elm bark box was probably something that he did every night.

"I will not wake up again," he said to himself after that second time. But he was wrong.

He had hardly drifted off to sleep when the sound of scratching against his little lodge made him sit bolt upright. There was still some light from the flicker of his small fire, and when he leaned his head close enough to his door to look through the cracks, he saw two little shadows poking about. One of them made a chirring sound and the other one chirped and growled in reply. Raccoons. He should have known that they would come. Of all the animals in the forest none were more curious.

One of the raccoons poked its nose right against the side of the lodge and began to climb up on it.

"Hooo!" Ohkwa'ri cried, making the sound of the horned owl.

The raccoon jumped down and disappeared as fast as a deerskin ball scooped up by a *Tekwaarathon* stick. Its companion scooted away almost as quickly.

Ohkwa'ri laughed silently as he listened to the sound of the two raccoons scurrying away through the dry oak leaves.

The next time he woke was when he had heard a strange sound. It was like the sound of regular footsteps. He listened and listened. An owl had been calling earlier, but now that sound was gone. From the other side of the great hills the lonely, unanswered call of a wolf had drifted to him once during the night, but that wolf had called only once. Even the wind, which had whispered its familiar song through the maple and oak leaves, was now holding its breath. Everything was completely silent.

Ohkwa'ri listened and listened. He began to realize that he was listening for things he could not hear. The small fire he had made in front of his new lodge had burned out long ago and so he could not hear the sound of it burning. Back in the big longhouse there was always the sound at night of the fires. Their hissing and crackling and popping noises were as familiar and reassuring as the nearby sounds of breathing from his family.

At night in the big longhouse he could always hear the sounds other humans make. He heard their yawns and their sighs. He heard the creaking of sleeping benches and the thump of hands or feet against the sides of the lodge when someone rolled over. He heard the sound of people when they woke and whispered to each other and laughed in a soft, knowing way. He heard the ones who woke and got up to place more wood on the fire in the winter when it grew quite cold before the dawn. He heard those others who woke when it was so warm in the summer that they would take a deerskin robe with them and go sleep outside near the longhouse wall. He heard the coughing that was so common in the late winter, especially on moist days when the smoke from the fires did not rise through the smoke holes but flowed around within the longhouse like a dry gray river. Those sounds filled every night, and the night was strangely quiet without them.

But there had still been that sound. Ohkwa'ri listened and listened. He could hear his own breathing. But that was not it. He listened further. *Blum-blump . . . blum-blump . . . blum-blump . . . blum-blump.* It was like the two-step beat of the water drum. Then he knew what it was. He was hearing the sound of his own heart beating.

The last time he woke, just before the dawn light, was when the light from outside his lodge grew so bright that he thought surely it was dawn. It was so bright that he pushed open the woven door he had propped in place and crawled out. There, looking down from the sky, was Grandmother Moon. Her full round face seemed as warm and caring as the face of his own grandmother. Her silver light made the river below him shimmer and gleam like a string of pale wampum beads. It was so bright that he could make out the shapes of the big longhouse and the other, smaller buildings of his own village on the far side of the river.

Ohkwa'ri stood and lifted his hands toward the moon.

"Grandmother," he said, "thank you for coming to visit me when I was feeling so lonely. You have reminded me what my mother taught me. Wherever I go, I will never be truly alone."

The light from the bright face of Elder Brother, the Sun, shone between the woven branches of the rough lodge door. Ohkwa'ri opened his eyes as those first rays of dawn touched his face. He felt cold and stiff. He had missed being able to stretch out to his full length, for his small round lodge was only big enough for him to lie curled up on the earth like a sleeping chipmunk. He lay there, breathing slowly, thinking about the night he had just passed.

As Ohkwa'ri walked down the hill toward the river, it seemed to him he could hear and see things better this morning than ever before. He was just a little tired from his wakeful night, but that night alone and going without a meal had sharpened his senses.

"It is just as my uncle Big Tree told me," Ohkwa'ri said to himself as he stopped to look at a beech leaf, seeing as if for the first time how its notched edges glittered in the sun, feeling with a finger the toughness of the leaf. "You are able to see better and hear better when you go without food for a time."

He remembered the story Big Tree told of the two young men who were always competing with each other. They both belonged to the Turtle Clan and so they were very stubborn. After they had both fasted for some days, each one tried to outdo the other with what he could see and hear.

"I can see the farthest hill," said the first man. "Can you see it?"

"Yes. I can also see the tallest pine tree on top of that farthest hill," said the second. "Can you see that?"

"Indeed I can," answered the first, "and I can see the highest branch on top of that tree."

"Ah," said the second man, "then can you see the butterfly resting on top of the smallest twig on that highest branch?"

"Of course," said the first man.

"I am now counting how many spots there are on its wings," said the second.

"There are six on each wing," said the second man.

"But listen! I can hear that butterfly's wings as they flap," said the first.

"Ah," said the first man, "I hear that too, but I also hear the butterfly breathing. Can you . . . ?"

But the two young men never finished their discussion. For at that moment their two mothers, who had walked up unheard behind them, each poured a cup of water onto the heads of their sons.

Now, as Ohkwa'ri walked, he began to hear a noise. It was a sound like an animal growling. He stopped and listened more closely, trying to figure out from where that sound came. It did not take him long, for the sound came from his own stomach. It was growling with hunger.

Ohkwa'ri patted his stomach.

"I am sorry," he said. "You are complaining because I have neglected you, my stomach. I left home without bringing any food with me. Now we will have to wait until I have crossed the river. But try to be quiet, my friend. A bear may hear you and think that you are another bear calling to him."

Ohkwa'ri smiled as he remembered how his father,

Two Ideas, had explained to him the way bears talk to each other. They had been walking in the woods for a long time and Ohkwa'ri's stomach had also been reminding him that it was past the time to eat.

"They growl like your stomach does, my son," he said to Ohkwa'ri.

His father was not always available to do things with Ohkwa'ri, for the younger sister of Two Ideas had several children, a son and two daughters. As a good uncle, Two Ideas had as much responsibility for helping with the upbringing of his sister's children as with the children of his wife. Thus, Two Ideas spent a good part of almost every day in the small Turtle Clan longhouse built just a spear's throw to the north of the great longhouse of the Bear Clan.

Ohkwa'ri did not mind. It was the way things were supposed to be. After all, his father and he were of two different clans. And it was that way with every father and son among the Longhouse People. You always had to marry someone of a different clan. That happened, as was right and proper, when a man's mother agreed with the mother of that man's future wife that the two young people should be allowed to marry. After the marriage the man would go and move into the longhouse of his wife's clan. And all children would belong to the clan of their mother.

Ohkwa'ri liked his father very much, and so he was glad that the longhouse where his father's nephew and two nieces lived was right next to their own. After all, his father would have been away much more often, going to teach things to his nephew. And his father had much to teach. For one, Ohkwa'ri's father was among the best hunters in their village. It was sometimes said that no one knew more about the ways of the animals than did Two Ideas.

As they walked that day in the forest, Two Ideas had talked to Ohkwa'ri about the bears. "You must always show them respect," he said. "Especially a mother bear who has cubs. Remember what happened to Grabber."

It was hard for Ohkwa'ri not to laugh out loud when he thought of how Grabber got his nickname. As a young man Grabber had thought very highly of himself. He wanted everyone to call him by a different name than the one he had been given by the midwife when he was born. He wanted to be known as Walks With the Bears. He had even taken the time and trouble to make a tattoo on his thigh that would stand for his name. He took a long time pricking his leg with a bone awl and then rubbing in wood ashes to make his tattoo. Most of the people had tattoos of one kind or another. Rubbing in the wood ash made the tattoos a beautiful blue color. But most people either had simple tattoos—lines, circles, curves like the shape of an uncoiling fern leaf—or asked the help of an older man or woman who was very good at drawing things to help them. This young man, though, was too proud of himself to ask for help. But he was not a very good artist. As a result the tattoo he made looked not like a man walking with a bear but like a very ugly porcupine leaning against a dead tree.

One day (before he became known as Grabber) that young man had decided that he would do something which no one else in the village had ever done. He would have a bear cub as a pet. So one fine spring day he set out from the village toward the place where the bears live to catch a bear cub. People shook their heads as they watched him go, but no one tried to stop him. It was widely accepted that one could never tell another person what they should or should not do. If they attempted to do something that they shouldn't, then they would learn soon enough why it was not a good thing to do.

It was not unusual for people in their village to have one of the animals of the forest living with them in their lodge. It was so commonly done that such animals would even be tolerated by the people's dogs. Usually those were orphan animals whose mothers had been killed in an accident or by a hunter. Such pets as raccoons and beaver were common and were regarded no longer as wild animals but as members of the family. Troublesome members of the family, at times.

A bear, though, was a different story, and stealing a young cub from its mother was not something that was advisable to try. So when that young man who wanted to be known as Walks With the Bears set out to catch a bear cub one spring, everyone in the village watched him go, and waited. They did not wait long. Elder Brother, the Sun, had traveled only the width of two hands across the sky when that young man came running as fast as he could back into the village, his eyes wide with fright, his hands holding onto his backside. He was shouting as he ran.

"The bear grabbed me! The bear grabbed me!"

He did not stop when he reached the village but ran right through it, right through the fields by the river, and right to the river itself. Perhaps he intended to run across the river too, but the water did not hold him up. Several people who had followed him pulled him out of the water before he could drown. The back of his loincloth had been torn by the swipe of a bear's claws and there were some deep scratches on his backside, but he was not badly hurt. From that day on, though, that young man became known to everyone not as Walks With the Bears but as Grabber.

"I am a hungry, hungry bear," Ohkwa'ri said as he listened to his stomach growling. As he walked down the rocky trail toward his canoe, which he had drawn up into the alders at the edge of the river, he wondered what food might be ready so early in the morning. His thoughts were divided between his hunger and his memory of Grabber's story. He began to walk faster as he thought of food. He no longer considered the possibility of danger. By the time Ohkwa'ri reached the place where the trail curved around a great stone to cross a rocky ledge, he was no longer watching where he put his feet.

Suddenly he heard a sound like pebbles being shaken in a hollow gourd. His heart leaped into his throat as he threw himself to one side to keep from stepping on the huge rattlesnake that was coiled in the middle of the trail. He landed hard on his shoulder. The rattlesnake was no more than an arm's length away from him. Its tail a blur of motion, it lifted up its head and looked at him.

Ohkwa'ri did not move. The rattlesnake's eyes were bright as crystals as it moved its head back and forth, flicking out its tongue. Then, deciding this reckless young human was no real threat, it uncoiled itself and crawled off the trail, disappearing into the rocks.

Ohkwa'ri sat up slowly. My sister is right, he thought. I forget to think sometimes. I will try not to be so reckless from now on. He stood up and began to walk again down the trail. This time he watched where he stepped. As he walked, he rubbed his bruised shoulder. I have learned a lesson, he thought. Then he shook his head and sighed. By now, he thought, the pot of food in our lodge will be empty. I will have to wait until later in the day to eat.

But when Ohkwa'ri reached over his canoe, he saw

two things. The first was a small basket made of birch bark filled with ripe strawberries.

Otsi:stia, he told himself, remembering that she had gone to pick berries at the same time he had left to build his new lodge. She must have crossed the river and placed these here for him before it grew dark last night. Thank you, my sister, he thought.

He lifted up the berry basket and picked up the second thing in his canoe. It was a pouch that looked just like the one his uncle Hand Talker had worn on his waist. He sat down, placing the basket of berries at his side. Then he opened the drawstring of the pouch and shook out its contents onto his lap. It was pemmican, smoked deer meat with maple sugar and dried blueberries pounded into it. Preserved by the maple sugar, food such as this would keep for a long, long time. And it was very good to eat.

Thank you, my junior uncle, Ohkwa'ri thought.

Plucking a trembling leaf from a nearby alder, he took a few of the biggest berries and a pinch of the pemmican and placed them onto the leaf.

"Little People," Ohkwa'ri said, "I am happy to share this good food with you."

He leaned over to place the leaf on the other side of the small alder's trunk so that the Little People could come for their meal without being seen.

He unhooked the bear-head drinking cup from his belt and went down on one knee next to the wide river. He leaned over where the rocks made a small pool at the river's edge and dipped his cup deep under the surface to get the cold, clean water near the bottom. Then, feeling happy inside despite his bruised shoulder, Ohkwa'ri sat back to enjoy his morning meal.

Part Two
The Defender

7

THE COUNCIL MEETING

Otsi:stia

*O*tsi:stia saw the canoe begin to cross the river and breathed a sigh of relief. She walked back up the hill toward the longhouse, not wanting her brother to know she had been up before dawn watching to see if he would come home safe and well.

It was not easy always being the responsible one. At times Otsi:stia wondered how her mother could remain so calm when having to deal with the foolish things that men always do. But this was not the time to think about the foolishness of men. Today there was something important to do. She began to walk straight toward the big longhouse, where she knew her mother and the other women were waiting.

When Otsi:stia reached the village, she saw that she had almost been too late. None of the women and men were in sight. The only person to be seen was a young man with a grim face standing guard at the entrance of the stockade of poles which surrounded the longhouses. It was Grabber. A newly made tattoo on his left shoulder, which looked like a very sick muskrat, was still red and swollen. Grabber now had put seven tattoos on his body, but he had still not learned how to do it properly.

Otsi:stia was sure that no one had told Grabber to guard the gate. It had been a long time since anyone had tried to raid their village. Perhaps a band of young men from some faraway nation to the south, seeking to do a great deed, might try to attack them to take captives. But this was not the time of year for such raids. And it had been so long since young men from their own village had gone out on such a raid that there were no other nations who felt they needed to try to even the score. In fact, the League of Peace was so strong that even the tribes who outnumbered the People of the Flint knew that any serious attack would be answered not just by one, but by all the five nations of the Longhouse.

Though Otsi:stia thought war was foolish and boring, she appreciated the fact that it had clear rules. She was very glad that any men who wanted to go to war always had to first gain the permission of the women and the men who were leaders. Because of that, they were now at peace with everyone around them, and they engaged freely in trade with the people toward the sunrise and toward the southland, the Anen:taks and the Mahicans and the Lenape.

Grabber, though, and a small band of other like-minded young men were not happy with peace. If there was fighting, Grabber might be able to make a name for himself. Even though he had been reprimanded by the men leaders for his plan to make a raid on the nearby Anen:tak village during the Strawberry Moon, she was sure that he still carried that plan in his heart.

Otsi:stia brushed quickly past Grabber. She did not like the way he looked at her. It was not certain, she thought, that Grabber and his friends would be taken as husbands any time soon. They had not been able to attract the attention of any of the young women, either in their own village or in their visits to other villages in the hopes that some young woman would take a liking to them and ask her mother to take marriage bread to the mother of that young man.

She was immediately greeted by Little Fox, one of the dogs that belonged to their family. Since this was not the season of the year for the men to go hunting with their dogs, the dogs were now often not around the longhouses. They went off in their own bands, coming home only when they were hungry or ready to sleep by the fires. But today Little Fox had not joined the others. Instead Little Fox had been sitting just inside the entrance to the stockade, watching Grabber and growling softly.

Otsi:stia leaned over and petted Little Fox, who wagged her tail, rubbed her side against Otsi:stia's leg, and then sat back down to continue staring at Grabber and growling.

Even our dogs know your thoughts, Otsi:stia said silently to herself. Then she continued on toward the big longhouse where the meeting was about to begin.

When Otsi:stia entered the longhouse, she was surprised to see Ohkwa'ri already sitting on one of the storage shelves above the sleeping benches in their section of the great building. Somehow he had gotten across the river and come up the trail to the longhouse before her. He must have come up the straight trail that led through the field planted with sunflowers that were already showing their pale green shoots. She noticed that he was rubbing his hand on his shoulder, which was scraped as if he had fallen on the trail.

Ohkwa'ri looked down at her, and then with a small smile, nodded. Otsi:stia understood. He had found the strawberries and was thanking her for them. It was not regarded as proper to make much of receiving a gift. The giver did not give the gift to be thanked for it, but because the giving was from the heart.

Otsi:stia looked around the crowded longhouse. Almost everyone was gathered there.

Big Tree stood, holding up the wampum which signaled that the council was to begin. As the keeper of the wampum it was his responsibility to care for it and bring it to every council, whether it be a small one like this, which was limited to their village; one of the councils between all three of the clans of the People of the Flint; or a Grand Council, which brought all of the clans and all five of the nations together.

The wampum would only be brought out during the day when a council was taking place. It would be put carefully away before the sun had set at the day's end if the meeting should last that long. It was not unusual for councils, even small ones, to take more than a day. A council was called so that the people could decide about something with one mind. Such decisions could not be made quickly, and everyone who needed to speak had to have a chance to make his or her opinion heard.

Otsi:stia's eyes were drawn to the wampum as her uncle held it up, draped across his upheld palm. The wampum strands were made of the spiral shells of freshwater snails, strung together on strings made of deerskin. This wampum was white, but sometimes the wampum shells were dyed different colors so that they could be put together on the strings in patterns. These could be used to carry a message, to help the people remember an agreement, or to explain a relationship between different nations.

Long ago, the story went, the people did not have wampum. But one day when Aionwahta, one of the founders of their League of Peace, was wandering, he came to the shores of a lake. That lake was covered with so many ducks and geese that you could not see the water. When Aionwahta came out of the forest, he startled the birds and they all flew up. They flew up so quickly that they took all the water from the lake with them. The lake bed was covered with shells, which Aionwahta picked up and tied onto rawhide strings. That was the first wampum.

Otsi:stia made her way through the people to climb up and sit next to Ohkwa'ri on the shelf above the sleeping benches. It was their favorite place to observe councils, and other children had taken similar perches around them and on the other side of the great longhouse.

"It is about *Tekwaarathon*," Ohkwa'ri whispered as his sister settled in next to him.

"*Henh*," Otsi:stia whispered back in agreement. She knew what the meeting was about. She combed her hair out with the fingers of one hand and then started braiding it.

Big Tree was ready to speak. He looked over toward She Opens the Sky, who sat with the other elder women across from the place where Big Tree stood. The Clan Mother nodded to him and Big Tree began. He started with the Thanksgiving Address, the first ceremony given to the human beings long ago when they received their original instructions. Everyone grew quiet as he spoke, his voice deep and calm.

"We join our minds together to give thanks to the Holder Up of the Heavens," he began. "Together we greet and thank our Creator."

"*Henh!*" the people answered with one voice.

Big Tree continued on. He expressed his thankfulness for the health and well-being of all the people gathered, from the Clan Mothers to the smallest babies. He thanked the Mother Earth for giving the people life. He thanked the living waters of the earth and the many plants, especially the Three Sisters—The Corn Maiden and her sisters, Bean and Squash. Each time when he paused, the people spoke their agreement, joining their minds with his. He continued on, thanking the birds and animals, thanking the Thunder Beings and the invisible beings of the four directions who are the messengers of the Creator. He thanked Elder Brother, the Sun, and Grandmother Moon and the many stars.

As he mentioned and described each part of the Creation, Otsi:stia listened closely. No matter how often she heard the Thanksgiving Address spoken, it always seemed new to her, reminding her of the purpose of, and the gifts given by, all the wonderful things around them. Hearing Big Tree's words, it seemed to her that even the grass must be listening.

At last the Thanksgiving Address was done. It had been spoken slowly and carefully and had left out none of the many living things that were everywhere. Now that the ground had been smoothed, they could begin to speak.

The man who had been delegated to speak about the ball game stood. His name was Wide Awake, and he was one of the Pine Tree Chiefs. Everyone knew him to be one of the finest ball players in all the five nations. It was right that he should be the one to propose that *Tekwaarathon*, the great ball game with sticks, should be played.

Wide Awake spoke simply and clearly.

"I bring forth the proposal that our village should play *Tekwaarathon*. It would be done for our elder Thunder's Voice, who is very ill. Perhaps this game will help him to regain his health, for when the people join together in this way, something good may come of it. It is right that we should play this game, for it is the Creator's game, a gift given us by the Creator. We are his children, and just as a parent looks on and is happy when he watches his children play, so too the Creator is happy when we play *Tekwaarathon*. And when the Creator sees that we have not forgotten the gift of this game, then he may also take pity and help heal the one who is ill."

Unlike some proposals brought to council, the decision on this was one that was, in a sense, already made. All of the people loved *Tekwaarathon*, the great ball game. It was played using the long-handled sticks with a net at the end in which a fist-sized ball made of deerskin packed tightly with deer hair could be caught and then carried toward the goal. Whenever there was a good reason—or almost any reason at all—such a game would be welcomed. In this case, though, the reason put forward by Wide Awake was the best one for playing the stickball game.

Otsi:stia knew that there were many ways to help heal someone who was sick. One way, of course, was by using the medicine plants. When an older person's bones were aching, for example, or they felt certain kinds of pain, then a medicine made of willow bark would help take that pain away. Sometimes people would doctor themselves when they felt such pains by plucking the soft tips of the young willow branches and chewing them. The juice in the willow would help clear away their pain and restore their balance. Health and balance was the natural way to be, the way the Creator intended things. Everyone knew that.

But healing often required more than just a simple medicine that one would drink or eat and rub like a salve onto one's body. That was because some sicknesses came to people because they were sent to them. If a hunter failed to thank the animals properly, then the animal spirits might send sickness to him. To heal such sickness would require not just a medicine but also the right ceremonies and words of apology.

Also, though Otsi:stia hated to remember it, there

were sometimes people whose minds grew so twisted that they deliberately sent sickness to others. Their jealousy and their bad thoughts gradually grew worse and worse until they had no love for other people, even though they might pretend to be normal human beings. Some of those people became witches and would bring death even to members of their own family. Otsi:stia quickly turned her thoughts away from that. Even to think about witchery was a dangerous thing, and she was glad that there was now no one in the village who seemed to have that kind of twisted mind. Grabber and his friends might be angry and even violent, but their anger was straightforward and their violence not the kind that would come in darkness.

She thought about the game being proposed, which would be done with all the people joined together in one mind to help Thunder's Voice. That was another way to help bring healing. When they played *Tekwaarathon* as a sacred game, it did not matter which side was the first to score three goals by hurling the ball so that it struck the post at their opponents' end of the field. What mattered was that the sick one—in this case the old, old grandfather known as Thunder's Voice—should know that the game was being played for him, in the hopes it would help bring him back to health and strength once more.

To see the people doing this for his benefit might clear away the clouds of depression that hung about the elder's head. It might wipe away the tears that had clouded his eyes since the death of his wife during the coldest part of the past winter. It might help him decide that it was not yet the time for his spirit too to take the long walk up the sky road to join those who had gone before him.

When Wide Awake finished saying what he had to say about the game, he sat back down. Others stood then to speak, each of them offering their own carefully expressed reasons for the playing of such a game.

Otsi:stia looked across the longhouse to make out the bent-over form of the old man, Thunder's Voice. He was sitting on his bench, farther down the longhouse. Though he did not seem to be listening to the words spoken, many of which spoke of him as a beloved elder whose health and happiness were important to all the people, Otsi:stia noticed that he seemed to be sitting a little straighter than he had the day before and that he did not seem to be leaning quite so heavily on the carved cane in his hands.

As the discussion went on, Osti:stia looked over at Ohkwa'ri. He was leaning eagerly forward, wanting to catch every word. It was not just that the content of the words spoken was good, it was also the way they were said. Two Claws, a tall, broad-shouldered man with a pattern of two blue lines tattooed down his face from his forehead, around his right eye, and to his chin, was now speaking. Those lines stood for the scratch marks made long ago on his face when he was attacked by a mountain lion and killed it. The scratches had healed, but the tattoo remembered his brave deed. Two Claws was also one of the Pine Tree Chiefs and had himself been a great player of the ball game, though his legs were slower now that he had lived almost fifty winters.

"The hawk needs two wings to fly," Two Claws was saying. "Now this elder is like a bird who has lost one wing. His heart is on the ground and it cannot lift up into the sky to come close to the sun. A bird which cannot fly is unable to sing and so his voice has grown quiet. It is right that we, the people, should lend him a wing. We should do so in a spiritual way by playing this game, so that he will know our love and our caring. He will see our people of all ages playing *Tekwaarathon* in a way which is meant to bring him back to a good mind and a happy spirit. Then he may feel his wing return to him, and with two wings he will be able to lift himself again from the ground and sing and feel the joy of life."

Otsi:stia smiled as she saw in her mind that healed hawk, which was the spirit of Thunder's Voice, fly again in balance. She noticed that the old man was sitting quite straight now and that he was no longer staring off into emptiness. His eyes were on Two Claws as he spoke. Even before the game was played, it seemed, healing had begun.

Although the discussion went on and on, when the

time came to make the decision, the council spoke as one voice.

"*Henh!*" they said. "We will have *Tekwaarathon.*"

Then Big Tree set the course.

"The game will be played tomorrow. It will begin here in the center of our village, and the goals will be set as we have set them before. The field will extend toward the sunrise in one direction and toward the sunset in the other. Each of the marker posts set at either end to mark the edge of our village will be a goal. The two sides will be these. We will not divide into sides by clan. Instead we will put the young men, those who do not yet have any children, on one side and the old men, those who have had at least one child, on the other. So it will be. I have spoken."

"*Henh!*" said all the people gathered, again voicing their agreement as one.

Otsi:stia turned to her brother, expecting to see a smile on his face. He was a fine player of *Tekwaarathon*. But Ohkwa'ri was looking over at Grabber and his friends and Otsi:stia realized why. How could her brother enjoy a game in which he was on the same team as Grabber's group?

8

THE SMALL PLAYERS

Ohkwa'ri

While his sister had been listening carefully to every word that was being said in the council, Ohkwa'ri had found himself already thinking hard about the game to be played the next day. Ohkwa'ri was the fastest of any of the other children who had fewer than twelve summers, and even as fast a runner as many of the grown men. When Ohkwa'ri played the ball game with the other young people in his age group, he was always the one controlling the ball. He tried, though, not to make it obvious. He was not the one who made all the goals. Almost always, when he had gotten ahead of everyone and was close to the goal, he would wait and then throw the ball to one of his teammates so that he or she could be the one to score.

The older people, who were always around when

the children played *Tekwaarathon*, would smile when watching Ohkwa'ri.

"He is like his uncle," they would say. "Big Tree played that way when he was a young man."

Ohkwa'ri had not yet reached his full height, but when he stood next to Big Tree, the boy's head reached his tall uncle's shoulder. His body still had some of the roundness of a little boy, but he was tough and strong. He was not afraid of being hit by the ball stick. That was good, because anyone who played *Tekwaarathon* and hoped to catch or carry the ball would surely be struck by the stick more than once. He would also be tripped, elbowed, and even trampled on if he fell. It was not uncommon for people to break fingers, toes, even an arm or a leg when a really good game was being played.

Even so, although he knew he would be allowed to play in the game on the following day, Ohkwa'ri was not sure that he would see much of the ball. Grabber and his friends Greasy Hair, Eats Like a Bear, and even the clumsy one called Falls a Lot loved to play the ball game. They would try to keep the ball among them so that the glory of scoring a goal could be theirs alone.

Although there might be as many as a hundred young men playing on their side, Ohkwa'ri knew that Grabber's group would bully their way to be in charge of things. Of course, they would also absorb a good deal of punishment from the other team as they played. However, even though they liked to push others around, none of those four young men were cowards. They were as tough as anyone in the village. Grabber was the finest runner and had never been beaten in wrestling. Eats Like a Bear was bigger than any other man in the village. He was able to lift up logs by himself that two people could barely budge. Greasy Hair was, next to Grabber, the fastest of all the runners in the village. Falls a Lot, though clumsy, could throw a spear — or a ball from his stick — farther than anyone else. It was sad that they were so proud.

If I were larger, Ohkwa'ri thought, I would not let them push me around. If I were older, I would try to teach them to respect others.

Ohkwa'ri sighed out loud. He was not older or bigger. He knew that tomorrow on the field he would be ignored by most of the older boys. Most of them were a little afraid of Grabber and his friends. They would not want to do anything to annoy them. And because it was generally known that Ohkwa'ri was a good player, they would be sure to keep him from doing anything that might draw attention from Grabber's circle.

Ohkwa'ri found himself remembering a time when he was a small boy of six winters. He had come into the lodge upset. Some of the boys were playing a game and had said that he was too small to join in.

His mother looked up from her work when Ohkwa'ri told her what had happened. She was preparing food as she knelt by their new hearth in the center of the great longhouse. The village had just been moved from its old place a short journey up-river, and she was still getting used to this new hearth. It was good, but somehow the old one had been better for cooking.

"Have you heard the story of the smallest ball players?" Herons Flying said to him.

"*Iah,*" said Ohkwa'ri. "No."

"Would you like to hear that story?"

"*Henh!*" said two voices. Ohkwa'ri turned around to see his sister Otsi:stia, who had followed him into the longhouse. Her face was filled with concern, and Ohkwa'ri knew she had seen her brother rejected by the bigger boys. But at the mention of a story the look on her face became happy.

Now, five winters later, Ohkwa'ri could still remember his mother's words clearly:

"Long, long ago the four-legged animals and the birds that fly decided that they would play a ball game against each other. It was agreed that the first team to score a goal would be the winner, and the field they set was a big one. One goal was at the place of the big falls toward the sunset, between the two great lakes. The other goal was at the place of the falls to the sunrise direction, near where our river runs into the river of the Mahicans.

"Before the game began, each team gathered to talk about their strategy. The animals met under a tall pine. The birds had their meeting in the top of a giant chestnut tree. Each side brought a drum to their meeting. You could hear the animals playing their drum and singing under the pine while the birds played their drum and sang in the top of the chestnut tree. Those songs were meant to inspire each side to play better.

"The birds had just finished their last song when they saw two small animals climbing up the tree. One of them was brown and the other one was black. Both of those small animals had big eyes. They were only a little bigger than mice, and they looked very sad.

" 'We want to join your side,' said the little animals.

" 'You do not have wings,' said Eagle. 'You must play for the four-leggeds.'

" 'They will not let us play,' said the two little animals. 'They say we are too small.'

"The birds talked it over and decided to take pity on the two little ones. 'We will give you wings so that you can play with us,' said the birds.

"Then the birds took their drum and trimmed off the two pieces of leather that hung loose on the outside of the drum. They fastened those pieces of leather between the legs of the little black animal. They had to stretch the leather to do it, and it was so thin that you could almost see through it.

"The little black animal, whose name was Bat,

jumped off the branch of the chestnut tree and flapped his new wings. Those wings held him, and he began to dart back and forth and up and down very quickly.

"The birds were pleased. But now they had a problem. They had used all of the leftover skin from the drum.

" 'I have an idea,' said the little brown animal. 'You could pull my skin on either side and loosen it.'

"Owl grabbed one side and Red-tailed Hawk grabbed the other. They pulled until the skin was loose on either side of the little brown animal's body. Then the little animal climbed to the highest branch of the chestnut tree and jumped off. He spread his legs out and glided across the sky until he landed on another tree.

" 'Now I am ready to play too,' said the little brown animal, whose name became Flying Squirrel.

"Then Eagle talked to those two new members of the team of the birds. 'Because you have just learned to fly,' said Eagle, 'you must hold back from the game for a while before you play. Watch carefully and you may see a time when you can help.'

"When the game began, the ball went back and forth but neither team could score a goal. Elder Brother, the Sun, moved farther and farther across the sky. It looked as if the game would end with neither side scoring a point, when Rabbit got the ball.

"Rabbit was so tricky as he ran that none of the

birds could catch him. As he went past the big chestnut tree, he felt himself growing tired. He threw the ball toward Fox, but his throw was high. A little brown animal leaped from the chestnut tree and spread its legs wide. It was Flying Squirrel. He swept right in and grabbed the ball in midair.

"Flying Squirrel glided over to another tree and scampered up to the top. Then he threw the ball to Bat. Bat went flying toward the sunset goal. The animals leaped and grabbed at him, but they could not catch him. Just as the sun went down, Bat, the littlest ball player, scored the winning goal for the birds."

Someone nudged Ohkwa'ri in his side. He had been remembering that story so well that he had forgotten where he was. His sister, who had poked him hard with her thumb, whispered to him.

"Listen," she said. "Thunder's Voice is going to speak."

Ohkwa'ri looked over toward the place where the old sick man had been sitting. He was surprised to see that Thunder's Voice was now standing. The old man's eyes, which had been clouded by his grief, now seemed clear. His eyes were looking right at Ohkwa'ri.

"People," Thunder's Voice said.

Even though he was very old, his voice was still deep and strong and it rumbled like the sound of the thunder from overhead. In fact, as he spoke, a roll of thunder sounded from above the longhouse. It seemed as if the Thunder Beings were answering the old man.

Then the rain began to fall very hard. It fell so hard that some of the women hurried to take long poles and pull the elm bark coverings over the smoke holes in the roof above them. The rain made a spattering, whispering sound as it struck the roof and the ground, and it was hard to hear anything else. But Ohkwa'ri did notice a very wet and unhappy-looking Grabber slip into the longhouse through its eastern door. Apparently he did not need to guard the entrance to their village when a hard, cool rain was falling.

"People," Thunder's Voice said again. His voice was so deep that it was easy to hear over the sound of the rain. "I would like to play in the game tomorrow. But I am too weak. I can barely walk. So I want to choose someone who will play in my place. I ask you to agree with me in my choice. Although he is young and does not yet have a child, I have watched this young man, and I know that he will play with a good spirit. I choose Ohkwa'ri to play for me on the Old Men's team. Do you agree with me?"

A loud *Henh!* answered his words. Almost everyone in the longhouse spoke that word of agreement. Only two did not speak. One of them was Ohkwa'ri, who had been stunned into silence. The other was Grabber, whose face was dark with anger.

Ohkwa'ri

After the morning meeting, Ohkwa'ri went out of
the village in the opposite direction from the river.
So much had happened so quickly. He was excited,
but he was also worried about the anger he had seen
in Grabber's face.

I need to find someplace away from the village
where I can be alone to think, Ohkwa'ri said to himself. He crossed the stony cornfield and began to
climb the slope of Big Nose, the hill over their village.
He stopped to look back and saw a small poplar tree
tremble slightly as if brushed by someone who had
stepped behind it to avoid being seen. He continued
to climb slowly. He wanted whoever was following
him to think that he was not aware anyone was behind him.

When he was near the top of the slope, he stopped,

turned quickly, and sat down. There was a noise below him like the sound of someone slipping and starting to fall. He scanned the slope out of the corner of his eye. A long stone's throw below him he saw several hands reach out and pull Falls a Lot, who had tripped onto his face, back behind a boulder where he could not be seen.

Ohkwa'ri stood up and stretched. He turned slowly and moved out of sight of those following him. This time, though, when he was out of sight, he began to run. He made a half circle, cutting off the trail and then slipping down the hill, stepping from rock to rock so that he left no footprints. Soon he was below the four young men who were following him. Hidden in the brush by the trail, he looked up and saw them ahead of him. They were still going uphill, following his tracks. They had sticks in their hands. The sticks were not ball game sticks. It was clear to Ohkwa'ri that they were intended to be used on him.

Ohkwa'ri crossed the river and climbed the hill to his new lodge. Tonight would not be a good night for me to sleep alone in my lodge, he thought. Grabber and his friends might come and beat me up. But he had left his ball stick there and needed to come and get it. When he reached the lodge, he took the *Tekwaarathon* stick and sat down on the hill to look at it. It was made of hickory, one of the strongest woods. He had played many games with that stick. Its handle was smooth from use. At the end the stick was bent into a half circle. The webbing of deer sinew fastened there had darkened with age. It was a good stick, but now Ohkwa'ri was worried. The stick was old, and there was a crack in it along the handle. It might break. Also, the stick was now a little small for him because he had grown so much over the last winter.

Ohkwa'ri stood up. He placed the end of his stick on the ground and held it against him. It only came up a little above his waist. To fit a man properly, his ball stick should be as high as his armpit. When Ohkwa'ri's people played *Tekwaarathon*, they did so holding their sticks with two hands. Their ball game sticks were bigger than those of any of the other four nations of the longhouse. This stick of his was more like the size of a stick that would be used by the Marshy Land People who lived toward the sunset.

Ohkwa'ri had intended to make a new stick for himself, but it was not something that could be done quickly. First a hickory log would have to be cut, and that was always done in the fall. Then it would be split into four pieces or more, using stone wedges and a heavy wooden club to drive them. That splitting would be done in the cold of the winter, when the tough hickory would be easier to split.

Next the stick would be roughly shaped and bent in two places, holding the stick over boiling water so that the steam would soften it and make it possible to bend it just right. Then the stick would be carefully stored to allow it to season. It would not be until late summer that the final work of shaping and smoothing the stick down would be done. The holes to string the lacing of the net would be made with a bow drill, and the stick would be oiled with bear grease. It took a full year to make a ball stick.

Ohkwa'ri sat back down and placed his stick on the earth in front of him. It was no use to think of making a new stick now. This stick was old and small, but it would have to do. He would have to put his mind into preparing for the big game on the following day. It would begin at dawn.

Ohkwa'ri cocked his head and put one hand up to cup it behind his ear. He could hear someone coming up the hill. He listened carefully. More than one person was coming. Perhaps Grabber and his friends were looking for him again.

As he listened, Ohkwa'ri decided that whoever was coming was walking quietly but not trying to be quiet. This was not the sound of people moving slowly and creeping up on an enemy. This was the sound of regular footsteps made by people whose walk was always quiet.

"*She':kon,*" a voice that Ohkwa'ri recognized called up to him. It was his uncle Big Tree. "Hello."

"*She':kon,*" Ohkwa'ri called back.

Soon Big Tree and the two other tall men who had come up the hill with him were sitting in front of the boy's lodge. Big Tree's hands were empty, but the other two still held the things they had been carrying. In Hand Talker's case it was a long bundle wrapped in pale deerskin. Ohkwa'ri's father, Two Ideas, was carrying a bundle of sticks in his powerful hands. Those sticks looked familiar to Ohkwa'ri. They were the ones that Grabber, Greasy Hair, Eats Like a Bear, and Falls a Lot had been carrying earlier. They had been broken into short lengths.

"Your new lodge is a good one," Big Tree said, putting his hand on the elm bark shingles which had been carefully placed so that each layer overlapped the one below.

Two Ideas put down the sticks next to Ohkwa'ri's hearth. He began to set them up to make a fire. "These sticks," he said, "were meant for you." He looked up and smiled at Ohkwa'ri. "I think you know that someone else was carrying them. When I met them on top of the hill over there," Two Ideas motioned with his chin toward the top of Big Nose across the river, "I told them that I would take those sticks the rest of the way. At first they did not agree." Two Ideas struck his big hands together, making a sound louder than the slap of a beaver's tail on the water. "However, after I talked to them a little, they agreed to give the sticks to me. Then they were in such a hurry to go to their homes that they fell down the hill. I think they are a little bruised now."

Two Ideas paused again and then went on, his voice more serious. "They are bruised, but not too bruised to play in tomorrow's game. It would be wise to watch out for them. Because of their little accident they may try to hurt other people when they play."

Hand Talker put his hand next to his head and made the circling motion to indicate that someone's thoughts were twisted. It was the hand sign the people used to indicate anger. Then he put his hand on his heart and extended it palm out toward Ohkwa'ri. It was the sign for that which is good. Ohkwa'ri understood. This meant that his uncle Hand Talker was thinking good thoughts for him. It also meant that he should keep his own heart good when he played *Tek-waarathon*. Then Hand Talker pushed the long bundle over to his nephew.

Ohkwa'ri unwrapped it. Even though he had guessed what it would be, his heart still jumped when he lifted it up. It was a beautifully made ball game stick. It was light in his hands. In fact, it felt as if it was pulling him up to his feet. He stood and made the motions of catching the ball, cradling it, and then throwing. He had never felt a stick like this one before. All ball sticks were alive, but this one had so much life that it felt almost as if it could play *Tek-waarathon* without him.

"This stick was made by your uncle Hand Talker," Big Tree said. "Hand Talker made it for Thunder's Voice three winters ago, but it has never been used. Thunder's Voice kept it stored under his bench in the longhouse. Now Thunder's Voice has given it to you. If you are to be an old man tomorrow, it is right for you to play the game with a stick that was made for an old man."

10

WATCHES EVERYTHING

Otsi:stia

*F*rom the place where she sat above the river-bank, Otsi:stia could see two canoes coming across the river. She was relieved to see that one of them was her brother's small canoe and that Hand Talker was in it with him. In the other canoe she could see their father and their other uncle, Big Tree.

It was Otsi:stia who had seen Ohkwa'ri leave the village earlier in the day and take the trail toward Big Nose. She had been sitting with her dog Little Fox on the big stone overlooking the trail, and her brother had not seen her. But Little Fox had growled and looked back toward the village. Then she saw the four young men following Ohkwa'ri, big sticks in their hands. They too did not see her, and she and Little Fox had rushed to find Big Tree and her father. As they trotted out of the village, she had seen Hand Talker join them.

Otsi:stia had gone back to her perch on the big stone, and soon after had seen Ohkwa'ri come down the trail that led from the back of Big Nose. She had smiled as he passed by. He had done a good job of doubling back and losing the ones who had been chasing him. But she, his sister, was able to keep her eye on him without his seeing her. It was hard for her not to laugh.

It was even harder for her not to laugh when Grabber, Eats Like a Bear, Greasy Hair, and Falls a Lot came limping down the trail. None of them were talking, and they walked as if they had been bruised in a number of places. None of them carried sticks.

Not long after that, her two uncles and her father came down the trail. When she saw the pile of sticks that Two Ideas carried, she could contain her laughter no longer. She laughed so hard that she almost fell off the stone. The three men looked up and saw her there. Big Tree nodded as he walked by. Hand Talker touched his hand to his heart and held it out in the gesture that all was well. Her father raised up one of those broken sticks and then laughed just as hard as his daughter was laughing.

By the time Otsi:stia was done laughing, the three of them were out of sight. She climbed down and followed them. But when she arrived at the longhouse, she did not see Ohkwa'ri and she did not see the men.

"If you are looking for Ohkwa'ri," her mother said, "I saw him crossing the field toward the river."

So Otsi:stia had gone down to the place above the river to watch and wait.

When she saw the canoes coming across the river, she ran down to greet them and helped Ohkwa'ri pull the elm bark canoe up onto shore. Hand Talker was holding two ball game sticks. One was beautiful and almost new. The other was the one Ohkwa'ri had always used. To her surprise, when they had finished pulling the canoe up high enough, Ohkwa'ri held out his hand and his silent uncle put the new stick into it.

"My sister, look at this stick," Ohkwa'ri said. There was excitement in his voice. He held the stick up above his head with both hands and then twirled it as if getting ready to make a throw.

Big Tree and Two Ideas had now pulled up the second canoe and were standing back with their arms folded. By the pleased looks on their faces Otsi:stia knew that something must have happened. She knew that she should wait and let them speak about it when they were ready. But even though she knew she would be teased for her impatience, she could stand it no longer.

"Tell me," she said.

Big Tree laughed. "My sister's daughter," he said, "we are going to have to give you a new name. Otsi:stia, 'The Flower,' is not a good enough name.

Maybe you should be called 'Watches Everything.' What do you think, my sister's husband?"

Two Ideas laughed. His laughter, like Big Tree's, was not at all unkind. In fact, it had an approving sound to it. "I think my daughter is much like your honored mother," he said. Then he paused, for it was not proper for a man to tease his mother-in-law or for her to tease him. "By this," Two Ideas said, no longer laughing, "I mean that my daughter is one of those who always seems to know what is going on in our village, just like her grandmother."

Hand Talker's laughter was in his eyes, but he was the one who answered Otsi:stia's question. He made the signs with his hand for storm clouds and for voice and for giving a present. Then he put his hand on the new stick. Otsi:stia understood immediately.

"Thunder's Voice has given you his ball game stick," she said to her brother.

"Henh," Ohkwa'ri said, trying not to sound too proud. It was important to always remain modest if you wanted people to respect you. "That is so."

Otsi:stia held out her hands and Ohkwa'ri placed the stick in them without hesitation. Otsi:stia was a good ball player herself, as were many of the girls and women. Sometimes the games of *Tekwaarathon* would be played in mixed teams, or on special occasions the men would play against the women. The women usually won.

Otsi:stia took a few steps, dodging, checking, scooping as if picking up an invisible ball. This *Tekwaara- thon* stick, even if it was a little long for her, was surely the finest one she had ever held. It was light, yet she felt its strength.

Ohkwa'ri watched and understood. Anyone who knew how to play the ball game would find it hard not to begin to imagine the game going on when they held that stick in their hands. That stick wanted to play ball. Perhaps the stick was even more eager to play because it had been wrapped up and put away for so long.

As Otsi:stia continued to move with the stick, her feet as quick and agile as those of a deer, the three older men exchanged a glance and then quietly moved away. They understood that Otsi:stia and Oh- kwa'ri would want to talk now.

At last, breathing a little hard, Otsi:stia spun the stick one final time and then stopped.

"I have given it a name," Ohkwa'ri said.

"That is good," said Otsi:stia, handing the stick back to him.

It was common for people to give names to such things as a ball game stick or one of the snow snakes, the spearlike poles that were used to play a winter game. In snow snake a trough would be made in the snow and then a snow snake pole would be thrown into the trough, so that it would shoot along on its belly. A good player could make a snow snake go very far down the trough. Eyes would be painted on the head end of the snow snake so that it could see its way and not jump out of the trough as it sped along.

"I thought of calling it Bat or Flying Squirrel. But then I had a better idea. I whispered it to my stick, and I felt it tremble in my hands. So I knew that the name was right." Ohkwa'ri paused. He ran one hand down the stick's smooth length the way he would pet a dog. "My stick's name is *Tase'hne,* The One Who Defends."

"That is a good name," said Otsi:stia. "I have an idea. Let us go find our mother's mother and I will tell it to you."

She Opens the Sky was standing on the small hill looking out with her keen eyes over the cornfields. She was deciding where more forest should be cleared for the planting that would take place next year. As the Clan Mother and the head of the Women Planters, she had to think far ahead beyond just one growing season. This was a very good place for their fields. Although there were many stones here, those stones held the moisture for the roots, and it seemed as if they made the soil better to feed the corn. She had tasted the soil herself and knew that the way it tasted was the kind of taste the corn roots preferred. It tasted even better than the dark soil close to the river.

Then she turned to look at Otsi:stia and Ohkwa'ri. Ohkwa'ri was holding a well-made *Tekwaarathon* stick. She Opens the Sky looked at that stick and Otsi:stia knew that her grandmother understood who had given the stick to Ohkwa'ri and why.

"Grandmother," they said, both of them speaking at once. *"She':kon,* we greet you in peace. It is good to see you strong and well."

"She':kon," she said, answering their formal greeting. "My grandchildren, I greet you in peace. It is good to see you strong and well."

The two children stood there without saying anything. They turned slightly to look out over the stony cornfield and She Opens the Sky looked with them. Otsi:stia noticed that she was as tall as her grandmother now. She Opens the Sky had noticed too, for she spoke words of thanks to the Creator.

"Holder Up of the Heavens, Creator, I send you this prayer. Thank you for allowing me to grow old. Thank you for allowing me to see my grandchildren grow tall."

"Henh," said Otsi:stia and Ohkwa'ri with one voice, adding their agreement to strengthen their grandmother's prayer.

They stood again in silence for a while.

She Opens the Sky pointed with her lips toward her favorite maple tree farther down the slope.

"Our Elder Brother, the Sun, is making it very hot here," she said. "Let us go and sit in the shade of that tree."

At the maple tree She Opens the Sky sat with her

back against the trunk. She had come there so often that the tree had grown to like her. Its trunk had shaped itself over the years to make her comfortable when she leaned against it, and it had grown a wide flat root right at its base for her to sit upon. Ohkwa'ri and Otsi:stia sat down by her feet. Ohkwa'ri was using the butt end of this new stick to make shapes in the earth near his feet. They looked much like two birds, yet they were not two birds.

Otsi:stia coughed. "Our grandmother," she said, "you know that tomorrow my brother will play *Tekwaarathon* as an old man."

"I know that, my grandchild," She Opens the Sky said.

"It will not be easy for my brother tomorrow. I know he is a good ball player, but he will be one of the smallest ones on the field. He will need help. So I thought of this way that I could help him."

Otsi:stia looked over at her brother. He was still looking down at the ground, at the shapes he had made with his stick. Without looking up, Ohkwa'ri spoke.

"Grandmother, you know the story of the ball game between the animals and the birds? It is a story that our mother told us."

"I know the story," She Opens the Sky said.

"In that story," Ohkwa'ri continued, "I think there are many lessons. But one of them, the one that my sister and I have been thinking about, is the importance of using your eyes well. The birds saw that the squirrel and the bat might help them, even though they were the littlest ones. And because the squirrel and the bat could see so well, even when it was getting dark, they were able to help."

"That is why we have come to you, Grandmother," Otsi:stia said. She unfolded the bundle she had been holding, and She Opens the Sky saw that it contained paints. "No one can draw pictures better than you can. We ask you to help us. It is very important to be able to see well when you play *Tekwaarathon*. So we ask you to paint a flying squirrel on my forehead, here above my eyes. We ask you to paint a bat on my brother's forehead. Then when he is playing, it will be as if I am with him on the field. My eyes and the eyes of the bat and the flying squirrel may help him to see better."

"Grandchildren," She Opens the Sky said, reaching out her hands to take the paints, "I will do this for you. I will give you the eyes of the bat and the flying squirrel tomorrow morning before the game begins."

11
BEFORE THE GAME

Ohkwa'ri

Ohkwa'ri looked up toward the smoke hole. There was still no sign of the light of dawn. He wondered how any night could possibly be so long, especially in this part of the year when Elder Brother, the Sun, stays the longest in the sky. It had not been possible for him to sleep, even with his new stick held in his hands.

"Tase'hne," he whispered to the stick, "Defender, soon it will be the day. Then we will play the game together. It does not matter if our side wins or loses, but I ask you to help me to play well. Help me to play in a way that is pleasing to our Creator, the one who gave us this sacred game. Help me to play in a way that will bring health to Thunder's Voice."

Ohkwa'ri sat up and swung his feet onto the earth. No one else was awake yet, it seemed. He made his way quietly over to the central hearth and sat beside it. He still held Defender cradled in the crook of one arm. He put his other arm out to hold his hand over the glowing embers, which were all that remained of the cooking fire from the night before. Soon people would be up. They would add wood to this hearth and to the other hearths up and down the big longhouse, and the good smells of wood smoke and of food cooking would fill the great building.

But now, Ohkwa'ri thought, pulling his hand back from the fire and grasping the stick again, I am the only one awake.

Even as he thought this it seemed as if his stick, Defender, grew warmer and moved in his hands. It was such a surprising thing to feel that it made him look to his side. Someone who had moved on very quiet feet was standing there in the shadows close by. Defender had warned him. But it was no one to fear. It was his grandmother. She came forward and knelt beside him. She held a large shell in one hand and a brush made of the hair from a deer's tail in the other.

"Grandchild," She Opens the Sky said, "it is good that you are up so early. Now I will not have to hurry as I paint your face. You want me to paint a frog on your nose, is that not right?"

Ohkwa'ri started to open his mouth to protest. Then he shut it. His grandmother was teasing him. He smiled at her with his eyes and she smiled back.

"*Henh,* Grandchild," She Opens the Sky said, "it will be a bat on your forehead."

"And a flying squirrel on my forehead," said Otsi:stia as she sat down next to her brother.

It was late in the morning when everyone gathered at the place where the game would be played. The two posts which were to be struck by a ball to make a score had been set up in the long stretch of meadow and woods along the river. The post were so far apart that when you stood at one, you could not see the other one. The game would be played through the woods as well as in the meadow, and there were no firm lines to either side, although the river and the hills which loomed above them served as final boundaries.

As Ohkwa'ri walked over to join those on his team, he looked at all of the people. Men and women and children of all ages were lined up on either side of the huge playing field. It was clear that word of the game had traveled fast and far. There were people gathered to watch the game who must have walked all through the night to reach the field. There were not only many people from the Turtle Clan Village and the Wolf Clan Village of their Flint Nation. There were also Longhouse People from the Oneida, the Standing Stone Nation, and from the Onondaga, the Firekeepers of the Great League, those who lived among the hills.

There were even some Mahican and Anen:tak peo-ple who had come from the lands toward the dawn to watch this game. Ohkwa'ri saw that some of the beautiful white Anen:tak birch bark canoes were pulled up on the shore below the village. He recog-nized the people by the strange way they dressed. One of them was especially noticeable, for he was very tall and he wore a headpiece made of the scalp of a bear. A necklace with many bear claws hung about his neck. Ohkwa'ri had seen that Anen:tak man before when he came to trade. His uncle Big Tree had told him that the man was a healer and that the costume he wore meant he specialized in bear medi-cine.

Although it was said that the game would begin at dawn, everyone knew it would not start that quickly. Elder Brother, the Sun, was said to be especially fond of *Tekwaarathon.* So a game would not begin until he was high enough in the sky to be able to see every-thing clearly. People also needed time to gather at the field, and the players needed to do the things nec-essary to be ready.

Ohkwa'ri walked around their village and watched what other players, young and old, were doing. Some were rubbing special oils into their sticks. Some were tying good luck charms around their necks and their arms and legs. Some were stretching and exercising or running back and forth to make themselves sweaty before beginning the game.

From a distance Ohkwa'ri saw Grabber and his friends. It was not only Eats Like a Bear, Greasy Hair, and Falls a Lot who were gathered together with Grabber this morning. Perhaps as many as twenty young men were sitting in a circle as Grabber spoke to them, telling them how they would organize their attack. Ohkwa'ri took special note of the young men in Grabber's group. Grabber was not the official leader of the young men's team, but it was clear that he was going to lead his own little team within the team. All of them had painted their faces like Grabber's, with one half of their face red and the other half chalky white. It would be easy to recognize them.

And, Ohkwa'ri thought, it will be easier for me to avoid being surprised by them during the game.

Ohkwa'ri knew that his team of old men included his father and other grown men who were aware of the fact that Grabber wanted to hurt him. They would do what they could to protect him. But they would not always be wherever he was. *Tekwaarathon* was a game that moved too quickly for anyone to always know where everyone was. Ohkwa'ri would have to defend himself.

"But you will help me," Ohkwa'ri said to Defender, shaking his new stick in front of himself as he walked. People were talking and shouting, but he could no longer hear what they were saying. His eyes were on the field, and his thoughts on the game about to begin.

The teams were gathering now near the center of the field. His uncle Big Tree was the one who would begin the game. He stood there, holding the ball and waiting patiently for everyone to be ready. It was a new ball, made of deer hair bound tightly together by a covering of deerskin sewed with sinew. It was the size of a man's fist and very hard. Players sometimes lost teeth or were knocked out when they were hit by a ball they failed to catch.

Everyone on the field was dressed much as Ohkwa'ri was dressed. Aside from charms to bring luck and the decoration of paint or tattoos, all that anyone wore was a tightly belted loincloth. Also some, like Ohkwa'ri, wore tightly laced moccasins, although there were many men who preferred to play barefooted. Such barefooted players did not have to worry about a broken lace or a torn moccasin.

Ohkwa'ri moved toward the place where Wide Awake, who was the leader of the Old Men's team, was gathering the players. Soon all of the Old Men, Ohkwa'ri among them, sat or stood in a series of closely packed circles around Wide Awake to listen to his idea. Some of the so-called Old Men were actually quite young, for one was called an old man only if he was the father of a child. The two sides would be evenly matched. Like a war raid, a game of *Tekwaarathon* would be carefully planned before it started. But, just like war, no one could ever predict what would really happen once things began.

"These will be our positions," Wide Awake said, drawing patterns in the soft earth. "This group will be like the wolves. They will be the first to see what is happening with the ball, and they will be in the middle of the field at the start. If we get the ball, they will be the ones to lead us."

Wide Awake looked about. The men in the group that would be like the wolves understood. When one went out to scout into dangerous territory, that person was sometimes called a wolf, for the wolf knows how to move swiftly and is always alert. Ohkwa'ri had been selected to be part of that group because he was such a swift runner. He looked around at the other men in his group, feeling proud to be among the leaders.

"This second group," Wide Awake continued, making further marks on the ground, "and the third group, they will be like the red-tailed hawks and the wide-winged hawks. They will sweep from one side to the other on the field behind the wolves. When the game begins, they will see who has the ball and then either move forward if we are attacking, or move back. As we have done before, they will go from side to side, but we will never leave one side of our field open."

Again Wide Awake paused. Ohkwa'ri noticed how all the men paid attention and no one spoke. These men had played *Tekwaarathon* many times and they understood the game. Although it might seem confused to someone watching who did not understand the game, there were always plans being followed.

"Our fourth group," Wide Awake said, "you are like the real bears. You are the ones who will stay the closest to our goal to guard it. This is the way you will play until the first goal is scored against us. When that happens and the ball is then given to us at our end of the field, look to me for instruction. I will have my hand raised high with my stick in my hand. If you cannot find me, look to Two Ideas. At some point in the game we will have our wolves and our real bears change their positions. That way neither group will grow too tired."

Wide Awake looked around the circles yet again. This time a few men spoke. They were experienced players, and they made simple suggestions or comments about what to expect from certain of the players on the Young Men's team. Ohkwa'ri listened closely to everything that was said. He had played *Tekwaarathon* before and watched the older men players more than once, but he had never been part of a game as large as this. There was so much to learn, even about the things that seemed the simplest. He had learned much in the past by watching the way the best players held their sticks or feinted with their heads.

"We are ready," Wide Awake said at last. He stood up and then struck the earth with the butt end of his ball game stick. It made a deep thump. He struck the earth again, and all the other men on the team of the Old Men did the same. This time the sound was so deep and loud that the earth beneath them vibrated like a drum. He began to move, shuffling his feet in a dance step, and the other Old Men moved in line behind him. Their feet added to the rhythm of the sticks that still thumped the earth. They were moving in a great circle that included all of the hundred men on their team. They moved calmly as they danced and struck the earth, but Ohkwa'ri felt the excitement that went around that circle. He felt the power too. It was not the thought of winning or losing that excited everyone. It was the desire that everyone felt to play this game well that filled their every movement with such strength.

They danced toward the side of the field where Thunder's Voice sat, and Ohkwa'ri noticed two things as they danced closer. He noticed that the old man was sitting even taller than he had been at the meeting the day before. And he saw that the eyes of Thunder's Voice were directly on him. Ohkwa'ri tried to hold his back even straighter as he danced, honoring the old man who had chosen him to play in his place.

Now Wide Awake sang. *"Hoh yah neh hoh yah neh."*

All of the Old Men dancing in the circle, which moved in the opposite direction from Elder Brother, the Sun, answered him. *"Way ho yah neh."*

The continued singing, their voices joining together with such strength that it seemed to Ohkwa'ri that everything in creation was singing with them. So they danced and sang their way to the middle of the field where Big Tree stood, waiting to start the game. He held the ball high above his head with both hands now. It was the sign that all preparations were over. It was the sign that *Tekwaarathon* was about to begin.

12

THE GAME

Ohkwa'ri

When Big Tree threw the ball high into the air, a great ululating cry went up from both the players and the many people watching. Some of the younger players watched the ball with their sticks raised, ready to catch it. But Ohkwa'ri was not one of those. He kept only one eye on the ball, and it was wise that he did so. Swinging his stick toward Ohkwa'ri's head, a slender young man with his face painted red on one side and white on the other sprang forward even before the ball began to arc downward. Ohkwa'ri hardly had to move his arms to lift up Defender, for his stick seemed to leap up to block the blow even before Ohkwa'ri saw it coming. Ohkwa'ri pivoted to one side and swung his leg so that the young man who had struck at him tripped and went flying onto his face.

Ohkwa'ri did not look back. Dust was already rising

around him, and people were shouting or grunting with effort. The rhythm of bodies striking bodies and sticks striking sticks was almost like the sound of music to him, and he knew he would have to move his feet in this dance or be danced upon!

He ran forward, staying well to the side of the wolves of the Old Men's team who had captured the ball as it came down and were passing it back and forth to each other as they advanced across the great field. It was not an easy passage. The players on both sides fought hard, and already several men on each side had limped or been dragged off the field. A broken stick and the churned-up earth behind them showed how fierce that first contact between the teams had been.

Ohkwa'ri did as his uncle had instructed. Although he was a wolf, he stayed back and did not get into the way of the larger, stronger men as they moved the ball. But his eyes were quick, and he saw his sister waving to him from the hill above the far side of the field. Otsi:stia—like many others not on the field—was running along the hilltop, keeping pace with the players. Ohkwa'ri was not sure how it was that he had known she was there. Then he remembered the bat and the flying squirrel painted on their foreheads. Perhaps their medicine was working!

Ohkwa'ri raised his stick in acknowledgment of his sister's wave. She gestured, and he looked where she was pointing. There was a clear space in the melee of men. He signaled back to Wide Awake, who was running behind the first line of men, guiding the play.

"*HIY, HIY, HIY!*" Ohkwa'ri shouted. It was the cry they had agreed upon to be given when a player saw a good opening. He pointed with his stick toward a weakness in the right flank of the defenders on the Young Men's team. Unlike the Old Men, they were not guarding the width of the field, but concentrating their strength where the ball was in play. There was an open lane there.

It had been Ohkwa'ri's idea that one of the players on his team would make his way to that opening. But that was not what happened. He saw Wide Awake rush forward, running with the long strides of a deer. Wide Awake dodged one defender, cross-blocked another to the ground, and then was given the ball. He ran back in the opposite direction, taking the Young Men defenders who were closest by surprise. Among them was a figure with a red and white face that Ohkwa'ri could tell, even from a distance, was Grabber.

Suddenly, to the surprise of everyone — especially Ohkwa'ri — Wide Awake turned and made a mighty throw of the ball. It flew through the air like a swallow taking wing, high above the heads of everyone on the field. As Ohkwa'ri watched it, thinking that he had never seen anyone throw a ball so far, he realized that the throw was aimed at him! By running backward Wide Awake had drawn everyone — except for

Ohkwa'ri—even farther away from that open flank.

Once again it was as if his stick had a life of its own. It seemed to quiver, and then Ohkwa'ri lifted it up to catch the ball, which struck so hard as it came down that it spun him halfway around as he started to run. He ran without looking back, so fast that many on the field could not tell where the ball had gone to, and headed for the place where it would have landed, rather than following Ohkwa'ri.

But the people watching the game knew where the ball had gone. Ohkwa'ri could hear many of them shouting and screaming encouragement to him. He heard the sound of pounding feet other than his own and looked to the side. Two other players on the Old Men's team were not far behind him, and he slowed to let them catch up. It was Red Duck, a burly grandfather who still was amazingly sure-footed, and Quick Eyes, a lanky young man whose first child had been born only a few days ago. Ohkwa'ri signaled with one hand that he would pass the ball to them.

No, Red Duck signaled back, go on. The two players spread out, one to each side of Ohkwa'ri.

Ohkwa'ri understood. They were not doing this to help him. They were doing this because he was representing Thunder's Voice in this game being played for the old man's health. He knew that close behind there were many men trying to catch up to them, but remembering Thunder's Voice made him feel stronger and more determined. So he did as Red

Duck urged and ran faster, cradling the ball in Defender's webbing.

They were passing through the woods now and Ohkwa'ri watched closely as he ran, weaving through the trees. It was well that he did so, for he saw the elbow of a member of the Young Men's team sticking out from behind an elm tree at the far edge of the woods ahead of them. Either someone had been too lazy to run the length of the field, or the Young Men had not been completely foolish and had posted at least one defender to wait in the forest. Ohkwa'ri gestured to Quick Eyes. Quick Eyes saw and crossed in front of Ohkwa'ri, heading for the elm tree while Ohkwa'ri swung away from it. The defender behind the tree leaped out, but was blocked to the side by Quick Eyes.

Now Ohkwa'ri was in the open field, and he could see the goalpost ahead. There was a pain in his side as he ran, but he did not slow down. There, standing not far from the goalpost, was a small group of people. Ohkwa'ri recognized almost all of them. One of them was Thunder's Voice. Clearly the old man, who was smiling broadly, had decided to take up his post near the goal that the Old Men's team would strive to reach. And there were Otsi:stia and Herons Flying. Both mother and daughter had their hands balled into fists as they shouted something. As Ohkwa'ri came closer, he realized they were yelling his name.

Behind them stood the tall Anen:tak man with the

bear headpiece. One arm raised in the air, he too was shouting Ohkwa'ri's name, though he was not pronouncing it correctly. Ohkwa'ri raised his stick high, darted in toward the goal, and struck the post with the ball, scoring the first goal for the Old Men's team.

There was little time to celebrate that first goal. The ball was carried back to the center of the field and was again put into play. This time the players surged back and forth, but no one side was able to quickly gain an advantage over the other. Elder Brother Sun moved the width of three hands across the sky, but still no further goals were made.

Although Ohkwa'ri ranged back and forth across the field, the ball did not come close to him. Still, he saw plenty of action, and there were bruises on his chest and a cut on one cheek from those times when he and other players came into contact with each other. He had been careful, though, to keep his eyes on the small group of players on the Young Men's team whose faces were painted red and white. It was not hard to watch them, for they were in the forefront of every play.

When the ball had been brought back to start the action after Ohkwa'ri's goal, he had seen Grabber looking at him. For a moment it almost seemed as if there was some admiration in the older boy's gaze, but then the look of anger clouded Grabber's face once more. Now Grabber was playing hard, playing as well as the best players on the Old Men's team. As

one of the old men made a throw, Grabber inter-
cepted it and threw the ball over to Eats Like a Bear.
Eats Like a Bear roared as he broke through the Old
Men defenders like a boulder rolling over a line of
saplings. The Young Men's team followed him. Ohkwa'ri, who had been struck in his stomach by someone's knee, found himself lying on the field. Red
Duck, who was limping badly and using his stick as
a cane, reached a hand down to help him up.

"Help me over to the side," Red Duck said. "My
right knee has just remembered that I am a grandfather, and it is ready to rest."

By the time Ohkwa'ri returned to the field, the ball
was already being thrown up to start play once more.
A spectacular goal had been scored by Grabber, and
the two teams were now even.

As the ball came down, the Old Men caught it, and
at a signal from Wide Awake the wolves and real
bears changed ranks. The play took the Young Men
by surprise, and the Old Men quickly reached the
woods in the middle of the field with the ball.

Ohkwa'ri followed. He had tripped as they changed
ranks and had the wind knocked out of him. Now he
was far back behind his teammates who had once
been the front line of attack. It was getting late in the
afternoon. Soon the game would be over. Then he
saw the place where a small rocky ravine cut into the
edge of the woods.

Ohkwa'ri ran toward that ravine. The men with the

ball had passed by there but had been careful not to come too close. The footing was treacherous and the slope was steep. Only someone who was a bit foolhardy would try to cut through there. However, Ohkwa'ri thought, if I am careful and I do not run headlong, I will manage to catch up with the others.

He looked up to the hilltop and was pleased to see that Otsi:stia was no longer in sight, though he recognized the tall figure of the Anen:tak man. He did not wish his sister to see him take this dangerous shortcut.

As Ohkwa'ri ran into the ravine, he kept his eyes open. He remembered how close he had come to stepping on the rattlesnake, and he knew this ravine too was a home for snakes. Defender throbbed in his hand, as if trying to warn him, and he held more firmly onto his stick. The edge of the ravine was now very steep and the slope pitched off to one side. If he fell here, he would surely do more than just bruise himself. Otsi:stia's words about being more careful echoed in his mind, and he became even more alert to everything around him.

It was that alertness which saved him. He heard the faint scrape of a moccasined foot on the path behind him. Without thinking, he ducked down low. Grabber's stick, which had been swung at the side of his head, brushed his hair as it whizzed past him like a striking hawk.

Defender throbbed in Ohkwa'ri's hand. As he

turned, still bent low to the ground, he thrust the butt of the stick into the pit of Grabber's stomach. The war cry which Grabber had just begun to shout ended with a loud *whoomph,* as the blow from Ohkwa'ri's stick knocked the wind out of the big young man.

Grabber stumbled back and placed one hand against the rock wall of the ravine. His red and white painted face was so filled with rage, it did not look like that of a human being.

"Grabber," Ohkwa'ri said, trying to keep his voice from trembling, "this is not *Tekwaarathon.* Let us go back to the field."

Ohkwa'ri's words did no good. Grabber lifted up his stick and began to swing it back and forth in front of him. "Ohkwa'ri," he said, in a voice that was more frightening because it sounded so emotionless, "you will not make a fool of me again." Then he leaped forward like a panther.

Grabber's first blow was so powerful that Ohkwa'ri felt his arm go numb as he blocked it. Grabber stepped back to give himself room to swing again with all of his force. They were close to the edge now, and Ohkwa'ri sensed the emptiness at his back.

Then, as the light of the day started to fail, Ohkwa'ri remembered the bat. The bat darts and flutters and no one can strike it. Ohkwa'ri feinted to one side and the other and then struck at Grabber's leg, throwing him off balance. Grabber swung his stick back, hitting Ohkwa'ri in the side. But the blow had little force to it, and as Ohkwa'ri stumbled back toward the wall of the ravine, Grabber suddenly disappeared from sight.

It had happened so quickly that Ohkwa'ri could not believe it was real. He blinked his eyes. There at the top of the slope was Grabber's *Tekwaarathon* stick. And there at the bottom, his leg twisted at a strange angle, was Grabber.

Ohkwa'ri went quickly down the slope, taking care that he did not dislodge any of the stones. The older boy looked up at him. The sweat that streamed from his forehead had washed away most of the red and white paint, and Ohkwa'ri could see clearly that Grabber was in great pain.

"Oh . . . oh . . . kwa'ri," Grabber said, his voice weak and confused. He reached out his hand.

Ohkwa'ri put his hand into Grabber's, but he did not pull him up. He could see that Grabber's leg was very badly hurt. As he fell, it had twisted beneath him and broken. The bone showed through the skin just above his knee, and the blood was starting to come pulsing out. With such bleeding, Grabber might die.

Ohkwa'ri let go of Grabber's hand and put both of his hands just above the place where Grabber was bleeding. Grabber groaned as Ohkwa'ri did this, but Ohkwa'ri did not remove his hands. Like all hunters, Ohkwa'ri knew how blood travels through the body, flowing in small rivers. He felt for the heartbeat in Grabber's leg, found it, and pressed there. The blood flow slowed.

"Do not move," Ohkwa'ri said.

Grabber reached out and grasped Ohkwa'ri's shoulder. "You . . . will . . . not . . . leave me?"

"No," Ohkwa'ri said. "Help will come."

But even as he said it, Ohkwa'ri was worried. He could feel his hands growing tired as he pressed to stop the flow of blood. Then, because he could think of nothing else to do, Ohkwa'ri began to sing. He sang a song that Herons Flying had sung to him when he was a very small child. It was the song to be sung when you were in need of a friend. And as he sang, he thought of the bat and the flying squirrel, the two friends who helped each other in the great ball game.

"Wey, hey yo, oh oh, wey, hey oh."

As he sang, his hands felt stronger, and it seemed as if, even in his pain, Grabber was less frightened.

Ohkwa'ri heard the sound of feet on the rocks. He turned and looked and thought he saw a bear coming toward them. He blinked his eyes and saw that it was not a bear. It was the tall Anen:tak man with the bear headpiece leaping agilely down the rocks to them. Close behind him was Otsi:stia.

The Anen:tak man pulled a pouch from behind his back. He took a cord from it and wrapped it about Grabber's leg above the wound. Ohkwa'ri removed his hands. The blood was not flowing. The Anen:tak man nodded at him.

"You . . . do good, Gwali," the Anen:tak man said. He took something from his pouch and placed it in Grabber's mouth. "Bite," he said to the older boy. Then he reached down and gave Grabber's foot a quick jerk, setting the bone back in place. Grabber's eyes opened wide and then he fell back in a faint.

13

THE VICTORY

Ohkwa'ri and Otsi:stia

The Old Men's team was singing as they danced around the fire. The Young Men's team, which seemed no less happy though they had scored one less goal than the Old Men, danced close behind them. Thunder's Voice stood watching them. The old man's face was calm and free of the worry which had been there for so many moons before *Tekwaarathon* had been played in his honor. All those around Ohkwa'ri were laughing. And more than one person came over to clap a hand on his chest in congratulation.

Suddenly a large figure loomed over Ohkwa'ri. It was Eats Like a Bear. He stood there, his eyes looking down at the ground.

"Ohkwa'ri," he rumbled. Then he stopped, as if uncertain what to say next.

Greasy Hair and Falls a Lot came out from behind

Eats Like a Bear, who was so large that Ohkwa'ri had not seen the two other young men at first. They too had embarrassed looks on their faces. It was clear that Grabber's friends had known about his plan to ambush Ohkwa'ri in the ravine.

"We have heard that you helped our friend when he fell," Greasy Hair said.

"Can you tell us how badly he was hurt?" asked Falls a Lot. "We have not seen him since . . . the accident. They took him to your grandmother's medicine lodge."

"His leg was broken so that it bled," said Ohkwa'ri. "But my sister was watching, and she brought the Anen:taks' healing man quickly. Grabber is strong. I am sure that he will be all right." *My sister was watching,* he thought, *even though I did not see her. Our medicine worked well indeed.*

"Henh!" Greasy Hair said.

"That is true," Falls a Lot added.

Eats Like a Bear reached out his large hand to pat Ohkwa'ri's chest.

"Ohkwa'ri," he said, "you played well."

Ohkwari reached up and clapped his palm against the chest of Eats Like a Bear. "You played well too."

Eats Like a Bear smiled and walked away with his two friends.

But Ohkwa'ri could not smile. All that he could think of was the way Grabber looked as he lay there at the bottom of the ravine. Grabber had wanted to hurt him, but Ohkwa'ri had not wanted things to end as they had. What if Grabber should never be able to walk again? What if he should die?

Otsi:stia stood apart from the crowd around the fire, her face as grave as Ohkwa'ri's.

"I know what is troubling you, my brother," she said softly to herself. Then she slipped away from the gathered people toward her grandmother's small healing lodge near the edge of the forest.

It was a long run to the place where Grabber was being cared for by the Anen:tak man and She Opens the Sky. Otsi:stia stayed at the lodge only long enough to find out what she wished to know. Then she turned and ran all the way back to the fire. It was not easy to locate Ohkwa'ri in the crowd, and when she found her brother she was breathless.

"Ohkwa'ri," she said, "it is all right. Our grandmother has told me that Grabber will not die. And if the Anen:taks' man is as great a healer as he says he is, then Grabber will be running again at the end of three moons."

For the first time since the fight in the ravine, Ohkwa'ri's heart felt light again.

"My sister," he said, "thank you."

A hand grasped Ohkwa'ri by the shoulder. He turned to look. It was Thunder's Voice.

"Ohkwa'ri," the old man said, his voice as strong as

it had been before his illness, "thank you for helping. All of those who played, both the Old Men and the Young Men, are part of this victory."

"Yes," Ohkwa'ri said, "the victory belongs to us all." And then he smiled.

EPILOGUE

*T*hree moons had passed since the great game of *Tekwaarathon* had been played. Ohkwa'ri walked down the hill from his little lodge. He had been sleeping there almost every night, but he was still not ready to give up his mother's cooking. Otsi:stia was waiting for him at the bottom of the hill. Her basket was full of blackberries. She looked up at her brother with pride, thinking how tall he had grown this summer. Best of all, though, he seemed to finally be listening to her good advice.

"Is our visitor still in the village?" asked Ohkwa'ri.

"Henh," Otsi:stia answered. "As usual, he is with his adopted nephew, but Ktsiwassos has promised that later today he will teach me how to make the poultice that draws out infection from a wound—the same one that he used for Bear's Son."

"That is good," Ohkwa'ri said. "I am sure that Grabber, I mean Bear's Son, would have died without that medicine."

Ohkwa'ri shook his head. It was strange how things happened. When the older boy was Grabber, he had hated Ohkwa'ri, but now, as Bear's Son, he showed Ohkwa'ri a grudging kind of respect. Bear's Son had once wanted to make war with the Anen:taks, but Ktsiwassos, the Anen:taks' medicine man, had saved the life of the angry young man once known as Grabber. He had even taken the young man as an adopted nephew. In return, Grabber had taken the name Bear's Son to honor Ktsiwassos, whose name meant "Great Bear."

"As soon as Bear's Son is completely healed," Otsi:stia went on, "he will make a trip to visit the Anen:taks' village."

Ohkwa'ri held the canoe steady as his sister climbed into it and then hopped in as he pushed it out from shore.

"My sister," Ohkwa'ri said, "it is as you said. One must think before one acts. Sometimes things do happen that you did not expect."

Otsi:stia looked at her brother with pleasure. "Ohkwa'ri," she said, "I am glad that you are listening to me. Perhaps when I am a Clan Mother, you will be a *Roia:ne.*"

Then Otsi:stia's laughter joined with that of her brother as the waters of their river lapped around them, singing songs of the changes and the seasons still to come.

AFTERWORD
The Village Has Returned Home

Although *Children of the Longhouse* is a novel, it is very much the story of a real place and real people. It is the result of a lifetime of learning from my Mohawk friends and neighbors. The personalities and ways of seeing the world that we find in the people of Ohkwa'ri and Otsi:stia's village are similar to those of many contemporary Mohawk people, whom I will not name, but who may recognize something of themselves in this story and smile. There is also some resemblance to the heroes and heroines in many of the traditional Mohawk tales that have been shared with me for more than three decades. In those stories, young men and young women overcome monsters and succeed against great odds through strength, courage, and unselfishness. There are many patient Mohawk friends and teachers I have to thank for showing me the way to those stories, such people as Tom Porter, Jake Swamp, Salli Benedict, Ernie Benedict, Mike MacDonald, Tehanetorens Ray Fadden, and his son, John Kahionhes Fadden.

I also have to thank the editors of the *National Geographic* magazine for commissioning me to write a story about a Mohawk village in 1491 for their October 1991 issue, a story I could not have written without extensive assistance from archaeologist Dean Snow. Although that story is quite different from this novel, it started me thinking about a more extended piece of writing based in that period.

Today the New York State Thruway winds west along the Mohawk River, passes the city of Amsterdam, and runs between the two great hills known as Big Nose and Little Nose. A Mohawk village was once on the northern bank there, in the shadow of the big hill. Corn was planted in the fertile ground among the rocks, and the people drank water from the hillside spring deep in the cleft valley, where rattlesnakes still live and the bears have their dens to this day. When the ground grew less fertile or the hunting was no longer good, the village was moved to another spot along the river valley, but eventually, it always returned again to that place. Archaeological evidence tells us that during the period of this novel, the late fifteenth century, a great longhouse and several smaller ones stood there, and that village was built on the site of several previous villages dating back more than a thousand years. Its name was Kanatsiohareke, The Place of the Clean Pot, and the modern village of Canajoharie drew its name from that older town.

The Great League of Peace and the representative system of governing in which women have such an important role was founded among the Iroquois nations well before the events in this novel take place. I hope that I have given a small sense of what that complex and democratic system was like, but I know my words have barely rippled the surface of the deep, clear waters of the Great League. I regard the tale of the founding of the league out of a period of chaos and bloody civil war—a bit like the contemporary struggle in the Balkan States of Europe—as one of the greatest and most hopeful epics of humanity, a tale of peace and true forgiveness. The words and the lives of contemporary Iroquois people are still inspired by that wonderful legacy.

Lacrosse remains the national sport of the Iroquois nations. You will find the names of many Iroquois people in the Lacrosse Hall of Fame in Baltimore. The concept of team sports as a whole—ball games from basketball to hockey—appears to have its primary origin in the pre-Columbian games played by the Native peoples of the Americas.

The story of Kanatsiohareke and the children of the longhouse does not end in the past. It continues today.

During the late eighteenth century most of the Mohawk people were forced to leave their beloved valley following the Revolutionary War in which many Mohawk people played a prominent role fighting on the British side. Although Mohawk men became world renowned for their ability as steelworkers and they helped erect many of New York City's skyscrapers, their only remaining land in New York State was a small reservation called Akwesasne, which straddles the Canadian border along the St. Lawrence River. There was a prophecy, though, that one day the Mohawk people would return to the Mohawk River Valley.

In 1993 that prophecy came true. After years of saving and fund-raising and seeking the right place, a five-hundred-acre piece of land was purchased at auction by a group of Mohawk people whose objective was to create a model Native community in their old homeland. It would be a place where everyone, whether Indian or non-Indian, would be welcome to visit, a place where the people would try to live in balance with the land, where their children would not forget to speak the Mohawk language. The place that they bought, in the shadow of Big Nose, which had been for some decades a county farm, is known again today as Kanatsiohareke.

Today, members of the Bear Clan, led by a gentle Mohawk visionary named Tom Porter, stand once more on land they know as sacred land. Once again the fields by the river are planted with Indian corn, and the people drink from that great spring, which never goes dry. Mohawk children climb Ohkwa'ri's hill, and the sound of the water drum Otsi:stia loved so well is heard on moonlit summer nights as the old social dance songs are sung. As it happened many times before over the centuries, the village of Kanatsiohareke has returned home.

SUGGESTED READING

Clanology: Clan System of the Iroquois by Sakokwenionkwas Tom Porter, North American Indian Travelling College, 1993.

Indian Roots of American Democracy edited by Jose Barriero, Akwe:kon Press, 1992.

Realm of the Iroquois by the Editors of Time-Life Books, Time-Life Books, 1993.

Tales of the Iroquois, Volumes I and II by Tehanetorens Ray Fadden, Iroqrafts, 1976.

Tekwaarathon, Akwesasne's National Game by the North American Indian Travelling College, 1982.

Traditional Teachings by the North American Indian Travelling College, 1984.

GLOSSARY AND
PRONUNCIATION GUIDE

ANEN:TAKS *(Ah-nen-dahks)*: Porcupines or Eaters of Bark, Iroquois name for Abenakis

DAGAHEO'GA *(Tah-gah-hey-oh'-gah)*: Two Ideas, Ohkwa'ri and Otsi:stia's father

GA-NA-WA-GA GA-HUN-DA *(Gah-nah-wah-gah Ga-hoon-tah)*: The River of Rapids; the Oswego River

GWEH-UH-GWEH-UH-GAH *(Kway-oo-kway-oo-gah)*: The Marshy Land People; the Cayuga Nation

HANIO *(hah-nyoh)*: Come on!

HENH *(heynh)*: Yes

IAH *(yah)*: No

IAKOTINENIOIA'KS *(Ya-go-de-nen-yo-ya'-ks)*: The Little People, literally "they throw stones"

KA-HU-AH'-GO GA-HUN-DA *(Gah-hoo-ah'-go Ga-hoon-tah)*: The Missouri River

KANATSIOHAREKE *(Gah-nah-jo-ha-ley-gey)*: The Place of the Clean Pot

KTSIWASSOS *(See-wah-sohs)*: Great Bear (in the Abenaki language)

NA-HO *(nah-ho)*: I have spoken

NE-AH'-GAH *(Nay-ah'-gah):* At the Neck; Niagara Falls

OHKWA'RI *(Oh-gwah'-lee)*: Bear

ONAWI':RA *(Oh-na-wee'-lah)*: The Tooth

OTSI:STIA *(Oh-dzee-dzyah)*: Flower

OYATAGERONON *(Oh-ya-dah-gey-lohn-ohn)*: The Cherokee People

ROIA:NE *(Low-ee-ah-ney)*: Good Men; the overall name for the primary body of men leaders

SHE':KON *(say'-goh)*: Peace, commonly said as a greeting

SHONKWAIATISON *(Shok-way-ah-dee-soh)*: The Creator

SHOSKOHARO'WANE *(Shows-go-hah-loh'-wah-ney)*: The Big Tree, one of the traditional Roia:ne names passed on from generation to generation among the Mohawk people

SKA'-NEH-TA-DE GA-HUN-DA *(Sgah'-neh-dah-dey Ga-hoon-tah)*: The River Beyond the Openings; The Hudson River

SKA-NO'-DAR-IO *(Sgah-no'-dahl-yo)*: Beautiful Lake; Lake Ontario

TASE'HNE *(Dah-sey'-ney)*: One who defends

TEKWAARATHON *(Day-gwaah-la-ton)*: Ball game; lacrosse

TE-UGE-GA GA-HUN-DA *(Tey-oo-gey-ga Ga-hoon-tah)*: The River at the Forks; the Mohawk River

WAHE' *(wah-hey')*: It is good